"Alana, can y

Locke wanted to m
probably a good th
her injuries.

She moaned. Locke gathered her closer to him and put his chin on her head. If someone had wanted to distract them, they'd succeeded. They had hit Locke in the place where it hurt the most and forced him to turn his mission from the president's safety to taking care of his partner. Because he was going to make sure Alana was safe.

Somewhere along the way she had become more important to him than his job, and Locke was never going to apologize for that.

As he looked down at his unconscious partner, Locke realized that if he was going to save the president, he had to set aside his feelings for Alana. If it could be used against him, then it was a liability. And liabilities cost him his job. If the president was killed because Locke was distracted by Alana, all of them would lose.

He had to let her go.

Lisa Phillips is a British-born tea-drinking, guitar-playing wife and mom of two. She and her husband lead worship together at their local church. Lisa pens high-stakes stories of mayhem and disaster where you can find made-for-each-other love that always ends in a happily-ever-after. She understands that faith is a work in progress more exciting than any story she can dream up. You can find out more about her books at authorlisaphillips.com.

Books by Lisa Phillips

Love Inspired Suspense

Secret Service Agents

Security Detail
Homefront Defenders

Double Agent
Star Witness
Manhunt
Easy Prey
Sudden Recall
Dead End

HOMEFRONT DEFENDERS

LISA PHILLIPS

HARLEQUIN® LOVE INSPIRED® SUSPENSE

Recycling programs
for this product may
not exist in your area.

LOVE INSPIRED BOOKS

ISBN-13: 978-0-373-45724-3

Homefront Defenders

www.Harlequin.com

Printed in U.S.A.

A father of the fatherless, a defender of widows,
is God in His holy habitation.
—Psalms 68:5

Thank you to all my Hawaii friends
for all your information, and my hubs,
who suffered through a research trip over our anniversary!

ONE

It was hard not to think about sharks, sitting on a surfboard off the coast of Hawaii. Secret Service agent Alana Preston could see the hotel, and the faintest hint of dawn reflected in the wall of windows as she bobbed up and down on the ocean. Soon enough she'd have to get back to her duties, but for now Alana intended to enjoy this moment and not think of sharks—or how so many of the humans she'd met had a bite far worse than the predators.

At least for an hour out on the water she could forget that she'd torn up her knee all those years ago and destroyed her chance to surf competitively. She could forget that she'd moved to the mainland to be a Secret Service agent. She could forget the fact that she hadn't called home since she left.

Working at the White House was everything she'd imagined and nothing like she'd thought it would be at the same time. She was exactly where she wanted to be: on the front lines of the Secret Service.

But Hawaii would always be home.

Alana was part of the advance team setting up for the president's impending visit, and though there was almost no time for anything but work, if her boss, James Locke, could make time for a morning run, she could surf. She'd seen the director leave the hotel in his running clothes and set out along the beach maybe forty-five minutes ago. Alana was the rookie on the team, which meant Locke would have his stern, chocolate-colored eyes on her until she could prove herself. Too bad every time he looked at her she wanted to squirm under his attention. Why did he have to be so handsome?

Not that anything was going to happen. She was way too busy proving herself, making it so that she was the kind of person her father would've been proud of. Alana looked over at the mountains, then to the shadow of the rest of Hawaii's islands on the horizon. *I'm almost there, Dad.* She was so close to losing the rookie title she could feel it. *I've nearly done it. Just like I said I would.*

She began to paddle even before her mind recognized the swell of the water. The minute she'd heard the surf report, Alana had brushed her teeth and dug out of her suitcase the board shorts and rash-guard shirt she'd always worn for surfing. No way would she waste waves like these.

Alana plowed through the water using her arms to propel her. When the moment came, she grasped the sides and hopped to stand as the surfboard cut through the water. The tunnel was beginning to form in front of her. If nature cooperated she might get in there for the ride surfers waited hours to find. There was nothing like the isolation of riding the tunnel of a wave. Cut off from the world. Invincible. Cocooned from everything. Free.

The board jerked. Alana's legs tightened on a reflex as something bumped into her from beneath the water. *Shark.*

It hit her again, jostling the board. She started to fall, a black-gloved hand grabbed her ankle and she hit the water.

The wave pushed her down. It happened sometimes, and even as it happened now, she already knew the momentum of the wave had forced her down. In a second it would pass and she would be free to swim up, but she still fought that encroaching panic. It'd been a while, but instinct kicked in. *Stay calm. Don't freak out.*

Where was the person she'd seen? Under the water it was almost completely black, and with the rush of the waves it was hard to even open her eyes, let alone find visibility for more than a split second.

Wait for the wave.

It would pass. Then she'd be able to swim to the surface and reach her next breath. She wasn't going to die down here in the cold black ocean.

Seconds that felt like hours passed as the wave made its journey to shore. A hand slammed into her and knocked her head forward. Alana choked on water and tried to swim against the current. Then she felt the hot sting of a knife glance across her middle.

Unable to wait any longer, she kicked out. Her foot hit something solid. Not the sandy bottom of the ocean. No, she'd hit a person. *He's still here.* She fought for the surface as two arms banded around her. She grasped at his arms, his wet suit, and then felt for his face. He wasn't using scuba gear. That meant he was holding his breath.

Which meant he would drown as well if he stayed down here long enough.

Alana renewed her fight. She wasn't going out like this.

Secret Service director James Locke ran for these moments, early in the morning when he could clear his head. Locke pushed out a breath and forced himself to run harder. He had a six-person team on this trip, but it was the lone woman who had all his attention.

He'd seen her on her board in the water. Then pretended he hadn't. Then felt like a moron for it. He would spot Alana Preston in a crowd, no matter what. She drew him, and Locke had been fighting the pull of his feelings for her since the first day. Still, he wasn't going to let the rookie distract him from leading his team and keeping the president safe. He had no time for a relationship.

With the hotel in sight, Locke's legs protested. He slowed to a stop, and a splash in the waves drew his attention.

A surfboard bobbed out of the water, but no rider followed. Then he saw a woman's arm. Alana's head broke through the surface. Another person emerged from the water, hair as dark as hers. A man. He grabbed Alana. She sputtered and screamed, then went back down.

Locke sprinted toward her. *Alana.* She was in the water, and she was in trouble.

He ran into the waves. Someone on the beach yelled. Locke replied, "Call 9-1-1!" Who knew what condition she would be in when he got her out? She might need a trip to the hospital.

He didn't want to think the worst. God wouldn't do that to him. Locke was going to pull her out, and Alana would be okay.

Water soaked his sneakers and his clothes up to his waist. Waves buffeted his torso and face, but he reached the spot where he'd seen Alana and dived under to try to find her. Locke moved through the dark wet, the cold. He'd never liked the ocean overly much. The water had too much power. It could dictate whether a person lived or died, and nothing could stop it when the waves were high and ready to swallow a person whole.

He found her. Where was the man, her attacker?

Locke lifted Alana out of the water and pulled her up so he could see her face, close to his. "Alana?" Her eyes were shut. She could almost be sleeping, but she wasn't. A wave crashed against them.

Locke raced back out of the water with her in his arms. A crowd had gathered. Someone said, "Cops are coming, and an ambulance."

Locke nodded but didn't take his gaze from Alana. He lowered her to the sand. She wore one of those shirts that surfers wore to protect their skin from being abraded by their surfboards. Across her left side, toward her ribs, was a wound. She'd been cut, but a reef wouldn't make such a clean line. It looked more like the work of a knife.

Her usually vibrant, tanned skin was pale. "Alana?" He checked for a pulse and then brushed dark brown hair, softer than anything he'd ever felt, away from her face. Her heartbeat was slow and faint. Was she breathing? He'd read her file. She'd been a champion surfer back in the day. He could see the scar on her knee where she'd had the surgery that had ended her career. But that was years ago. Why had she been the target of an attack now?

His breath came fast, even as his thoughts raced. He couldn't think what to do. She had a pulse. Was she breathing?

A lifeguard ran over. "Everyone back up." He wasted no time performing mouth-to-mouth.

She isn't breathing. Locke held his breath until he

saw her jerk. The lifeguard turned her to her side, and she coughed seawater onto the sand. His eyes filled with hot tears, enough that Locke had to walk away or she'd see. She could be dead, and it would be his fault.

He couldn't go through that again.

He studied the crowd. These people were early-morning surfers, beachcombers and dog walkers. Not the kind of person who would have tried to hurt his colleague. None of them were even wet. Beyond the crowd a man in a black wet suit ran across the beach from the shore toward the hotel. No scuba gear. Had he dumped it in the water?

Locke jumped up, pushed through people with a brief "Excuse me" and kicked up sand as he tore across the beach as fast as he was able.

The man ran with a knife in his hand, taking the tool of his trade with him. Straight but uncombed black hair, short on the sides and shaggy on top. Asian.

Locke didn't even have a gun, which made it tricky if he was going to confront the attacker. He never carried his phone when he ran, or his keys or wallet.

The sand switched to concrete as he hit the walkway at the edge of the beach. He skirted around an elderly couple on an early-morning stroll hand in hand, then pushed his pace harder as the man raced to a parked Toyota. A rusted-out wreck with open windows and nearly bald tires. What kind of getaway vehicle was that?

"Stop!"

The man was almost at the car, so Locke yelled again, "Secret Service. I said stop!"

Wet suit guy dived across the hood. A head popped into view as the driver sat up in the front seat, which had been tipped all the way back. This second man wasn't in a wet suit. Not even a shirt, but he wore a white shell necklace. *Surfer dude.* Older, though, in his sixties, as far as Locke could tell. Caucasian.

And he almost looked familiar.

The man scrubbed his face with his hands and brushed long graying hair from his eyes. Combined with the dark shadow of stubble on his chin, Locke couldn't get a good look at his facial features. His friend yelled, "Drive!"

The car engine sputtered to life as the knife-wielding man got in the passenger seat. Locke memorized his wide-set eyes and flat nose.

The car sped away. No license plate, but he wasn't going to forget either of the men.

Alana sucked in a full breath of salty sea air and moved to sit up. Someone put a hand on her shoulder. "Easy."

She blinked, and the man came into focus. An EMT. "What…?" She didn't have the energy to get more words out than that. And why did she think Locke should be here, standing among the crowd of people and a grim-looking lifeguard?

Alana waved off the pressure cuff and sat up. A sharp stab in her side hitched through her like she'd been nicked at exactly that second. "Ouch." She touched her waist and felt the slit in her rash guard. When she brought her hand away, her fingers had blood mixed with sand on them. She'd been injured surfing before, but never like this.

A black-gloved hand.

"He grabbed my leg."

Locke pushed through the crowd. "The perp drove

away with a friend. Old car, no plates." He stood over her in his running clothes, his wet shirt clinging to his dark skin. His eyes were filled with concern.

"You went in the water?"

He shrugged, not happy. "I had to get you out."

Like that was supposed to be obvious to her? She was in trouble, so he'd retrieved her. No big deal. Alana sighed and let the EMT help her to her feet. She swayed a little, and the EMT held her steady. Not the man she wanted, not the one who would never give her even one indication he might feel the same way she did. Locke kept things completely neutral between them.

And then he jumped in the ocean to save her.

But that wasn't what she wanted to occupy her thoughts with right now. As they walked she glanced over her shoulder at Locke. Her colleague shook the lifeguard's hand and then brought up the rear with the second EMT, who carried a bulky bag.

The EMT beside her said, "We'll get you to the bus and patch up that cut. See if you need stitches."

Alana shook her head. "I won't." Not to mention she didn't want them to call in the local cops. No way. She'd been avoiding that since she got here, and intended to escape the island unscathed by the wrath of her brother. Seeing Sergeant Ray Preston wasn't on her to-do list.

The EMT didn't seem to believe her, so Alana said, "I'm serious. I've had a lot of surfing injuries—reef rash, jellyfish. I know cuts, and I know this one isn't deep enough to need stitches."

Locke's voice cut over whatever the EMT had been about to say. "He's still going to check it out, Preston."

Great. Now they were back to last names—hers at least. Everyone called him Locke.

Alana wanted to roll her eyes. She *hated* when he called her Preston, like she was just another one of the guys. A growl emerged from her throat, but she tamped it down. The EMTs didn't need to know she was mad.

"Wait." The EMT slowed for a step. "Preston? Alana Preston?"

"Yeah." Alana said it on a sigh. He probably knew her brother.

"No way! My sister thought you were aces. Still does. Kept all her old surfing posters of you. She has the board my dad got her one Christmas that matched yours. She never went surfing, though, just kept it in her room. She's graduating from U of H this summer. She's gonna be a vet."

"Awesome." She shared a smile with the EMT, though the thought of a younger sibling hitting a milestone was bittersweet. She hadn't seen her sister, Kaylee, either. Not because she didn't want to. It was Kaylee who'd told her she never wanted to see her again.

And the last time Alana had seen her brother, Ray hadn't been much nicer than that.

Alana climbed in the ambulance and lay down on the stretcher. Her fingers wouldn't stay still, no matter how much she squeezed them together. Hopefully Locke wouldn't notice. Was he going to file a report? Dumb question. Of course he was—with the police *and* the Secret Service. Her reaction would be noted, and that note would go in her file. She had to act calm. Cool. She needed something to think about other than the black glove as it gripped her ankle and pulled her into the water.

Locke stood just beyond the step, arms folded across his lean chest. What was he mad about? Was it the attack—like that was her fault—or the EMT knowing who she was?

Maybe he didn't like the fact the other man knew she'd been a competitive surfer. It wasn't like she hid it, though she didn't talk about it too much. It was in her file, but it was unique to her and people often asked her about it. Occasionally she'd meet a fan of hers from way back, like this EMT and his sister. And why not? She'd done something not many people had. Why did Locke have to be such a downer about it?

Alana wasn't going to back down. "What's up with—" The EMT wiped her injury, and she gasped. "Ow. That hurt."

Locke's frown shifted into an almost smile. It was about as much of a smile as he ever gave anyone, so she counted it as one. Because she was acting like a baby instead of sucking it up like a real Secret Service agent? She didn't know why that would be funny.

"I'm not saying sorry." The EMT kept his gaze on her cut. "But you're right, it isn't bad." He slapped cream and some gauze over it that he taped down. "All done."

"Great." She shifted to the edge of the bed. The quicker this was over, the quicker they could get to their morning meeting. They'd be late if the police took too long taking her and Locke's statements.

Locke held up one hand. "Not so fast."

"What?"

"He's right," the EMT said. "You've gotta keep that dry. Take care of it, or you'll have to see a doctor."

Locke shook his head. "That isn't what I meant." His gaze zeroed in on her, and she didn't like it one bit. "Someone just tried to kill you."

TWO

Locke ignored the bright Hawaiian sun and threw the car in Park outside the residence they were due at in ten minutes. He couldn't believe Alana was brushing off what had happened to her. It was like she didn't even care, or was trying to prove to herself she didn't care.

They'd stopped for coffee after giving the police their statements and going to the morning briefing. At the police station, Locke had looked through mug shots trying to identify the men he'd seen. While he'd been searching fruitlessly through the police's database, Alana had chatted with every cop in the building like they were old friends.

And yet every time the door had opened, she'd clammed up. Was she on edge because she'd been attacked, or was she not so excited at the prospect of seeing her brother? Ray Preston was a police sergeant, but he hadn't shown up. Maybe he didn't want to. Still, Locke figured it was just a matter of time before he did.

Maybe those cops had been old friends of hers. And maybe jealousy wasn't ugly like he'd thought, but that was probably just Locke kidding himself. He should probably just tell her he was attracted to her so she could tell him that no way on earth would she fall for her uptight team leader, and then he could move on with his life.

That would surely be easier than wondering for a split-second what might have been, followed by convincing himself that dating in this job was the worst idea—which it was.

Locke sighed. They had a lot of work to do before Air Force One's arrival, and she'd promised that if she needed a break she'd tell him. What else could he ask for? Still, she acted like it was no big deal that she'd nearly died, while Locke could barely breathe he was thinking about it so much.

Who was that Asian man who'd targeted her? Why try to kill her in the ocean? The police had issued a BOLO for both the car and his description of the two men. Locke wanted to be out looking for them, but they had Secret Service duties to attend to.

He glanced at her, pleased her color had come back, at least. He motioned toward the house and decided it was time to test the rookie. "Tell me about this one."

Locke didn't miss the face she made. Alana glanced up from the iPad in her lap and looked around at the street he'd parked on in Wainaku, just off the beach on the other side of the island from their hotel. On screen was the file she'd been reading over.

Alana frowned and then shifted in her seat to look out the back window. She wore black pants and a light blue blouse now, her hair pulled back. No earrings— they could get caught on something if a situation occurred. If he hadn't seen it just hours ago, he wouldn't think she had nearly died that morning. But she had, and he couldn't forget it.

"I rode my bike this way to get to school." Her Hawaiian heritage showed in the almond color of her hair and those peaked eyebrows. She was beautiful—not that Locke had made a point to notice. She was both his subordinate and five years younger than him. Even if he had time for a relationship women were too much work, and he had a president to protect.

Keep telling yourself that.

Alana said, "Does Beatrice Colburn live here now?"

She looked lost in childhood memories. "What does the file say?"

"House number is 456. It's the right one." Alana paused for a moment. Locke didn't even try to figure out what she was thinking.

He grabbed the door handle on his side. "Let's get on with this."

They had visited three people since the briefing. Beatrice was the fourth, and it was still early. Before POTUS landed at Hilo airport, they had to visit anyone who'd ever been flagged by the Secret Service's intelligence division. Anyone who'd written a threatening letter to the president was entered into a file. If they had the means or the inclination to actually carry out the threat, they were of particular interest to the Secret Service.

"Tell me what you learned from Beatrice's file."

"In 1977 Beatrice Colburn wrote a series of angry letters to the then president after her boyfriend was killed in Vietnam. The threats were directed at the office in general and not at President Ford specifically. As a high school chemistry teacher, Beatrice was deemed a viable threat because she had the knowledge to carry out her stated intentions, as well as access to the materials necessary. She was also fired from her job."

"And your assessment?"

"She's a retired supermarket manager with a deep tan who visits the library once a week and checks out six books at a time. She takes Krav Maga classes, and her four dogs are each champions in agility competitions. This is an active woman with a busy life enjoying the time she has now." Alana pressed her lips together. "I find it highly unlikely she's going to attempt anything against the president during this visit."

She locked the iPad screen and got out of the car.

Alana met him on the sidewalk, and Locke went first. Not because he wasn't a gentleman, but because he would never allow a woman, or any subordinate, to stand in front of him on the job. He was the first line of defense for any threat.

He stopped at the front door. "So why are we here?"

"Because we have to ask her what her intentions are, and she has to tell us that she plans to stay far away from the president."

Locke nodded, once. "She'll have cookies still warm from the oven. And lemonade she made fresh this morning."

Alana blinked and then smiled. "Seriously?"

He knocked on the door. "We develop a rapport with these people on each presidential visit. It's procedure, but it doesn't have to be boring."

Every time he knocked on a door, Locke held his breath. At this point it was habit, but after an anarchist had shot at him and his partner through the door his first year as an agent, he felt that same hitch with every visit. The echo of that shot so many years ago, a boom that had him diving to the ground. It had never left him. He still had scars on the outside of his arm to remind him that being careless never turned out well.

Barking erupted from inside the house. There was a crash, and a woman screamed.

Locke tried the door handle, and it opened. He drew his weapon and glanced back at Alana. "Right behind me."

She had her Sig out also and gave him a short nod. The times he saw her business face instead of the easygoing, relaxed Alana who hung out with the team were few and far between. He should have been pleased to see it now, but instead he missed that spark in her eyes.

The hall was the same yellow paint and linoleum floor as it had been the last time Locke was here. The door was open, as were all the windows in the place, letting in the morning breeze. He cleared each room from front to back, where the bedroom was. Dogs raced in circles around his feet and barked. Locke nudged his way through. "Beatrice?"

He reached the bedroom doorway. Beatrice Colburn was on the floor. Her shirt matched the hall paint, which leached the color from her skin, now a gray pallor. Locke slid to a halt in something sticky that covered the floor and saw the man in the window, sitting on the frame—half in, half out. The same man Locke had chased at the beach that morning.

The assailant's gaze hit Alana, and he started. Surprised by something.

Locke and Alana held their weapons on him. The guy had an intricate tattoo on the inside of his left forearm and a bloody knife clasped in that hand. His right hand was holding a roll of paper big enough to be a poster. Or a painting.

"Free—"

The man dived out the window.

"Stay with Beatrice," Locke said over his shoulder. "Call for backup and an ambulance."

Locke raced to the window and climbed out. He didn't want Alana anywhere near the man who had tried to kill her this morning. The window frame snagged a thread on the pants of his new suit. He grimaced but cleared the window to land in a bush and then raced across the backyard through the open gate.

Thunk.

The sound reverberated in his skull. He'd been hit from behind, blinded for a second as pain set off like fireworks in his head.

Locke landed on one knee on the concrete. The perp shoved him down so that he fell prone and ran past. Locke reached out for the man but grasped nothing. He aimed his gun from his position, then blinked as his vision split the man into three and back to one. Locke got up and ran after the guy. A sidewalk rimmed the house, and his shoes clipped the concrete with every step. Locke held his weapon up and traced the wall of the house with the other hand.

The man raced to a mustard-colored Cadillac parked two doors down and jumped in, still holding the rolled-up yellowed paper. No license plate on the back of this vehicle, either. The engine turned over, and the guy peeled out. Locke pulled out his phone and snapped a photo of the car before it turned the corner.

Hearing sirens in the distance, he went back inside. The dogs weren't any calmer, so he herded them into the kitchen and shut the door before he strode to the bedroom. "Is she…"

Beatrice Colburn lay on the floor, two bloody fingerprints where someone had touched her neck to check for a pulse.

"Alana?"

She emerged from the bathroom, a tissue balled up and pressed against her mouth. She lifted it away, her face pale and clammy. "Beatrice is dead."

"And you've never seen a dead body before."

It was a guess more than a question, but she didn't want to talk about it. "I'm okay."

She didn't look it. Locke put his hand on her back and led her to the living room. "Sit for a minute. If you can handle the dogs, get yourself some water. I'll show the cops in."

She'd gone through selection and training, and now the sheen was wearing off. Long days, round-the-clock protection, stress and physical strain. Sure, they were in most people's ideal vacation spot, but this was so far from a fun trip it was almost sad. After two years working together Locke was still wondering if she was going to last as an agent.

She lifted her chin, but her lip trembled. "I'm fine, Locke. I just needed a minute."

No one called him James. His mom and his friends from back home called him Jay. He wondered what it would sound like coming from her lips. He knew she didn't like the rookie moniker, but everyone had been a beginner at one point, even him.

What he said next would be a big test. "That was the same man who tried to kill you this morning."

Police sirens sounded right before two black-and-whites pulled up. She didn't answer him; instead Alana rushed to the window. "Oh, no."

Alana sucked in a breath to get that smell out of her nose and shook out her head, her shoulders, her arms…all the way down to her hands. It was a technique she'd learned to combat the fear that surfing—especially competitively—brought. Shake the feeling off and then get on with it anyway. But a dead body? Not something she wanted to see again any time soon.

A black glove. He grabbed her foot.

And now her brother was here. There wasn't even time to catch her breath. Locke had already gone outside to greet the officers, one of whom was Ray, but she needed a second before she faced him. Alana unclipped her phone from her belt. That attack was *not* going to slow her down. She'd seen the tattoo. Beatrice's killer, the man who had tried to kill Alana, too, was Japanese mafia. Pulling up old numbers, decades old in some cases, she sent a text to a guy she'd gone to high school with. Everyone knew Mikio Adachi's father was the yakuza boss on the Big Island, the head of the Japanese mafia. And even if things had changed since she left, Mikio would likely still know something about a yakuza soldier and why he might've tried to kill her.

The text sent, so she stowed her phone away. A long shot, but if it paid off she'd tell Locke about it. She knew this island, these people, but that didn't mean she needed to rub it in everyone's faces. Coming home wasn't exactly turning into a pleasant experience.

Alana looked around, then realized she was standing alone in a dead woman's living room. She circled the beat-up coffee table, brushed the dog hair off her back that she'd picked up from sitting on the couch and walked past the tasseled lamp to reach the door. Locke had the front door open, so she went out.

Two cop cars, three officers. One was the sergeant she'd been avoiding all day. They were huddled around Locke—the Secret Service director, the team leader. Mr. Never Wrong. Suit and tie.

She knew it wasn't all that easy being the boss in a job like theirs, but the man seriously needed to lighten up. She wanted to know what he looked like in board shorts. Alana would have a lot of fun teaching him to surf—as if that would ever happen in a million years. She caught the snort before it came out and cleared her throat. Much better than thinking about this morning, or what Beatrice looked like lying on her bedroom floor.

Locke turned. "This is my partner, Agent—"

"I guess you couldn't avoid me all day."

Alana stared down her brother, unwilling to give him the satisfaction of knowing he was right. Thankfully he hadn't been at the police station that morning when she'd gone there with Locke to give their statements about the attack on her.

"Can we not do this, Ray?"

She couldn't look at Locke. Alana was supposed to be a professional, a success. He couldn't know she was such a disappointment to her family. Her brother had been her biggest supporter, at every one of her surf competitions. He'd been crushed when she was injured so badly she had to quit. She'd kind of thought that becoming a Secret Service agent would prove to him she could still do something good, but evidently not.

Her brother didn't back down, his dark eyes disapproving over that flat, wide nose she shared with him and their sister. "Went surfing this morning, got yourself hurt."

Deep down, below where he could show it, her brother cared. Alana had figured that out, despite his lousy way of exhibiting any feelings whatsoever. She could have brushed off his comment, but instead she said, "I'm okay." Alana didn't know how to bridge a gap that spanned years. "Ray—"

Locke broke into the conversation. "The same man was here. Same knife, probably. He killed Beatrice Colburn and stole something."

No one said anything. The tension was so thick she could have cut it with the shark tooth her father had given her. Locke probably had no idea what was going on, and she wasn't about to explain it to him.

Ray's jaw twitched. She could tell he didn't like the fact she'd been close to a killer, one who'd hurt her already. "He saw you?"

Alana couldn't answer that in a way her brother would like.

Locke said, "I caught up with him. He hit me and got away." He touched the back of his head, and his fingers came away with a spot of blood.

"He hit you?" He hadn't told her that. She'd probably already given herself away, with that reaction, but she couldn't go to him. Ray would see right through it.

Locke pulled out a handkerchief and pressed it against the back of his head. "It didn't hurt until I touched it." He gifted her a tiny smile.

Alana stared at the curve of his lips. Ray cleared his throat, and she spun around.

One of the officers, an older man, came over. "Joe Morton. I worked the job with your father."

Alana nodded, shook his hand. Her father had been shot one night during a drug deal gone bad. Cops had been called in, and some guy hadn't wanted to come quietly so he'd shot her father only a few years before he was supposed to have retired.

Dad had been dead before she and her sister could meet their twenty-two-year-old rookie-cop brother at the hospital. Two weeks before her eighteenth birthday. Six months after her dream of being a champion surfer died when the doctor told her that even after her knee healed, she'd never get her edge back. Worst year of her life, and the catalyst for her seventeen-year-old sister screaming at her to get out and never come back. The upside of that being she hadn't had to see the disappointment on her brother's face every single time he looked at her.

Locke cut through her spiraling thoughts. "Let's get inside and get to work. Sound good to you guys?"

The cops moved toward the house, but Locke intercepted her. "We'll be there in a sec. Let you secure the scene first." When the two officers and her brother had stepped in the house, he turned to her. "You okay?"

"Sure, why not?"

His black eyebrows lifted. "Because that was your first dead body. And because you were attacked this morning. And apparently that police sergeant is your brother."

"I don't want to talk about Ray." She wasn't going to explain that it wasn't her first body, though maybe seeing her father in the morgue didn't count. "I can help, you know." She folded her arms, careful not to stretch the cut on her abdomen. She just didn't want to be in her brother's space. "I'll search the basement."

"Very well."

She rolled her eyes, but he didn't see because he'd unlocked his phone and was making swirly patterns on the screen. They walked inside and he showed the drawing on his phone to the first cop, Joe Morton, who'd worked with her father. "Any idea what this means?"

"Huh." He scratched his chin, and his gaze drifted to her. "Looks to me like it might be yakuza."

"Japanese mafia?"

Ray strode in. "Show me that." He took Locke's phone before Locke could hand it over. "It's yakuza. But then, Alana would know that."

She didn't rise to it, even though he was intent on baiting her. "We went to school with a few of them." She turned to Locke. "It is yakuza."

"Were you planning on telling me this?" Great, now Locke disapproved.

"If it turned out to be significant, yes."

"If…" Locke actually sputtered. It was kind of amazing to hear him at a loss for words. And why did it please her so much? Being in the same room as Ray and Locke was messing with her head.

"I'm gonna go check the basement."

"I'll go with you," Joe Morton offered.

"No, I will." Locke's voice stalled both of them. Alana mushed her lips together to keep from objecting. She turned to the cop. "Maybe next time, Joe."

The basement wasn't a big room. Workbench. File cabinet. Not a man cave or some kind of old lady knitting or crafting space or anything like that. There were schematics printed on huge sheets of white paper and framed on the wall. A lamp had been shoved over, and the shade was crumpled. The outline on one wall where a painting had hung was now just a void. The frame lay bent on the floor with broken glass.

Much better than thinking—or talking—about a dead woman. Or her brother. Or the glove, and the sting of that knife. Alana was sad for the loss of life, but she could hardly process what she'd seen in the rush of everything. Was it going to hit her later? She hoped not. She didn't want to know what that would feel like.

However, and whenever, it happened, Locke *would not* be there.

Behind her, he said, "Oh, no."

She spun to Locke, who said, "That frame, the roll of paper he was holding. It must have been this."

"What?"

He looked up. "Schematics for a bomb."

THREE

Alana stepped back from him. "That was on her wall?"

Locke nodded, fully aware that things had now escalated. "She kept it as a memento. I didn't really understand it, but she showed it to me every time I came. Wanted to talk about the old days when she could say what she really felt. But it was pretty harmless." He sighed. "The yakuza soldier who tried to kill you came here to kill Beatrice and steal this."

Alana looked at her phone. "No reply, not yet." She told him about the text she'd sent—to the yakuza boss's son, of all people.

Locke looked around one more time. "Okay, let's head back upstairs and tell your brother what we suspect the man took. We need to wrap this up and make our last visit."

"There's one more?" She climbed the stairs behind him.

Locke didn't turn around. "The marine, former sniper—" Something clicked in Locke's brain as two thoughts coalesced. Was the Caucasian man he'd seen in the beat-up car their next visit? Could their day be that connected? If it was him, the man's appearance had changed a bit since Locke had last seen him, so Locke couldn't be sure until he saw the file.

He said, "After that we're done for the day. Just in time for lunch."

"I don't think I'm going to eat for a week." She paused. "But what was that about the former sniper?"

"I just need to look at his file when we get back in the car. That's all." Then he would know for sure whether it was the sixty-something guy he'd seen that morning.

She nodded, and it didn't seem fake. She was actually holding up pretty well, and he was proud of her. He'd figured they would run across her brother at some point, but hadn't known the sergeant was Ray until she'd confirmed it. Alana had been through a lot in her life, and now this on top of it. Did she have faith to fall back on? There was something in Alana that helped her hold it together, even now. He thought it might be pure strength of will. Unless all that bravado was just for show. Locke couldn't tell yet which it was.

He, on the other hand, had been born and raised in Chicago, and his family had gone to the same church his whole life. Christmas wasn't Christmas if he didn't make the trip home to attend the carol service. Locke's father was still the CEO of the same company he'd started forty years before. Two older sisters, the youngest of whom was six years older than him. Private school. College paid for by his dad. He'd seen a presidential detail at the age of eight and decided then that protecting the president was exactly what he wanted to do with his life.

This was the path God had put in front of him, and until Alana showed up, he'd been completely satisfied. Being a Secret Service agent took one hundred percent of his focus and attention. It was everything he'd always wanted. He'd been convinced this was the best, the only way to be a good agent. Had relied on it, in fact. Now when he saw how Alana tackled everything, it made him wonder if she was destined to fail trying to cope without relying on God for strength.

Or if he was the one who was wrong about everything.

Ray was crouched over the body of Beatrice Colburn. From the doorway Locke explained what they'd found in the basement.

The sergeant nodded but didn't look at Alana. "You were right. It was a stab wound to the inside of her arm. The medical examiner will have to confirm, but if the cut severed her brachial artery she could have bled out in thirty seconds." He looked at his sister. "It was precise. And intentional. If I'm right, then he knew what he was doing. There wasn't anything you could've done."

Her brother cared, though Locke had never seen a sibling act like that with another sibling. It was like they didn't even know how to communicate with words—just the sentiments that went unspoken between them. He shuddered to think what it would be like if they were forced to talk about their feelings with one another.

Alana wandered over to the cop who knew her father, Joe Morton. The man was scrolling through the victim's cell phone. Probably looking at Beatrice's call and browser history. What apps she had that might give them a clue why the yakuza killed her.

Locke needed to call the other director, William Matthews. His colleague was lead on the team traveling in with the president, while Locke was lead on the advance team. Coordinating made both of their lives easier, as would their being friends. Had they actually *been* friends. Locke respected him fine and they'd worked together a long time, but he didn't particularly like the man.

Alana had requested to be on William's team for this trip, but Locke had made sure she was on his. As much as she would rather downplay her background he needed her expertise and her knowledge of local people to aid their team on this trip.

As she wrote down the numbers Morton was also noting, Locke dialed William. He was glad Alana had turned her attention to something practical, even though they weren't part of the murder investigation. It would keep her mind off seeing her first dead body.

"Matthews."

Like he didn't know it was Locke calling. "William, it's Locke." He bypassed the pleasantries neither of them had any interest in exchanging and told William about the dead woman, the yakuza guy who'd tried to kill Alana and the missing bomb schematics.

There was quiet on the line, and then William spoke in a low voice to someone he was with.

"Can you hear me?"

"Sure," William said. "Seems like a crazy coincidence, the two of you stumbling on a breaking and entering gone bad. Is Agent Preston okay?"

"Alana is fine." He saw her turn and smile at him, but he didn't believe it. Nor did he believe William's concern was simply that. More likely the man was playing defense—determined nothing would interfere with the President's trip, least of all a break-in. "I'm a little more worried right now about the fact this guy stole bomb schematics."

Alana's brow crinkled, and the smile evaporated off her face. She turned away. It wasn't his job to make her happy. She was going to have to work that out all by herself.

"Yeah, crazy. Bomb plans are probably worth something on the black market. People will buy anything off the internet." William's voice quieted, and he spoke again to someone he was with. "I'm interested to know this guy's angle. Think the local police will find him?"

Locke said, "I'll be going over there again with Alana to look at mug shots of yakuza soldiers. We'll figure out who he is, then the cops can pick him up. Guess we'll unravel this, and this morning's attack on Alana, somehow."

Would her brother help? The man could be a valuable ally if he wanted to be.

William said, "That's the police's job, Locke. You're not their director, so make sure you go see their captain and get approval for anything you do in their jurisdiction."

Locke wanted to roll his eyes but had practiced the art of resisting that urge from the age of four. William spoke like he was Locke's director, or at least someone he reported to, instead of his colleague. "I'll take care of it. And I'll file the report."

"Report?"

Locke said, "This needs to be passed on. A woman on our intelligence list is dead, and the man who killed her stole schematics to a bomb designed with the purpose of killing the president."

"Like I said, it's nothing but a coincidence. Even if your killer was going to construct the bomb from archaic plans he stole, he could be planning to...kill a wild pig with it. The president? That's a stretch."

Locke ignored the man's sarcasm and said, "It's a

stretch I'm supposed to make." That was their job—
to see the threat no one else saw and take appropriate
steps to neutralize it. Or if there was no other choice, to
give their lives to protect the president. Locke stepped
outside. "I cannot in good conscience ignore a possible
threat. You know that, William."

The other director laughed. "Alana was right. You
are too serious. It was a break-in, some small-time theft
gone wrong. Unless there was something left out of your
explanation that proves this to be a legitimate threat to
the president's life?"

As if things were ever that cut-and-dried. "It was the
same man. I've explained that."

But that wasn't the part of William's speech that
had caught his attention. Locke was still stuck on what
Alana had said about him to William. He turned back
to the house and glared but couldn't see her. Maybe
that was why she had wanted to be on William's detail.

"If it escalates, we'll take care of it." William sighed.
"For now, do what you will, Locke. I'll be there on Air
Force One tonight."

William had already hung up, so Locke tucked his
phone back in his pocket. At least he thought this could
be a real threat, regardless of what other people's opinions of him were. How the attack on Alana was connected remained to be seen, but his phone call with
William had only cemented the fact he was alone, just
like always. He would work to keep her safe, but Alana
was his subordinate—and nothing more.

"Thanks for distracting me with this, Joe." Alana motioned to her phone and the list of numbers she'd typed
into her notes app. Incoming and outgoing calls Bea-

trice had received on her cell phone. Nothing jumped out at her, probably just cold callers and friends Beatrice wanted to talk to. Likely the information wouldn't yield a reason why the yakuza had killed her.

"Tell you a secret?" He leaned closer. Alana shrugged. He said, "I don't like dead people."

"Neither do I." She set her hand on his arm. "I'd much rather be surfing."

"You got that right, sista." His expression changed, and she caught what it was about when he said, "Seen Kaylee since you been here?" Totally innocent, like he wasn't trying to father-figure her while Ray was in the room. Her dad had left a hole in her life she hadn't even begun to figure out how to fill in the years since.

Alana made a face. "My sister wouldn't answer the door even if I did go over there. Kaylee made it clear she didn't want to see me again. Ever."

Joe made a tut sound with his mouth and shook his head. "Shame. I heard—"

"Agent Preston." Locke's voice was a bark.

Alana turned to her colleague. Boss. Whatever. She pasted a smile on her face. "Yes, Agent Locke?" It just sounded weird to call him that. The whole team called him Locke, and she didn't know what his first name was. Surely it had been mentioned when she first met him, but she couldn't remember. It was bizarre to think of calling him something else, anyway. Like he had a personality instead of just a buttoned collar and tie, shiny shoes and a gun.

"We should make our last visit for the day."

Right. The marine sniper, the one Locke had wanted to check the file for.

"And that's my cue to leave." She looked at her

brother. When he didn't say anything, she decided to go for it. "'Bye, Ray."

He muttered, "Sounds familiar."

Locke touched her arm, and she went with him. They were so different, and yet she felt more at home with him than with her family.

Alana wasn't going to apologize for her brother, no matter how much dichotomy there was in her life. Things were what they were. Alana didn't regret leaving, but she did regret what things had become. If she could prove to Ray what a good Secret Service agent she was, then he'd see that it had been the right decision for her to leave for the mainland.

Locke turned the vehicle on and got the air-conditioning running, but didn't pull away from Beatrice's house. Instead, he grabbed his iPad from the back seat. "It's him. I knew he looked familiar. I just couldn't place him."

"Huh?"

He looked over from the screen, and tilted it in her direction so she could see the photo. Clean-cut, green fatigues. "The sniper. It's the man I saw in the vehicle this morning. Our yakuza suspect's getaway driver. Though he looked a lot more like a beach bum, with long hair and a beard."

Locke drove them to the last house, through the forest reserve to a deserted stretch of mountain. Dirt trail, so much foliage they could barely get through. The SUV would probably get scratched up on both sides.

"Are you sure this is the right direction?" Alana swiped through to a map on the iPad but couldn't get a strong enough signal for it to tell her where she was.

"I've been here before, remember? It was years ago,

but this isn't an address you forget." Unlike the man's face. Though years ago Brian hadn't had facial hair—or looked like a beach bum.

"And this guy—" she found the man's personal information "—Brian Wells? He lives here?"

"Yes. And if I take a wrong turn, I'll tell you. I'm not one of those guys you women complain about who can't ask for directions. There's no point driving around in the middle of nowhere and getting lost."

Alana shifted in the seat. What had *that* been about? It was bad enough being alone in the car with him for hours. Especially now that she knew he only cared about work. Okay, so she'd kind of known that already, but sometimes when he looked at her there was this…flash. That was all, just this spark on his face, or in his eyes, that said there was more than just work under that staid business demeanor.

She really hoped there was something else. Otherwise the man had a very boring existence. Not that Alana's life was better, but it was a whole lot more interesting. And when she proved to everyone that becoming a Secret Service agent was what she was born to do, they would know it had been the right choice.

The foliage on both sides crept back, away from the car, over the next few feet as the road widened. Heavy leaves stretched toward them, great palms that bowed low when the rain she'd been caught in so many times hiking poured from the sky. Those camping trips years ago that had been rained out were some of her best childhood memories. Alana had gone all over the world in the last year on protection detail as a Secret Service agent, and before that she'd been assigned to several different US cities. But she'd missed her home state.

They emerged into a clearing, someone's front yard. The house was an old Airstream with bricks instead of tires that had probably been there for fifty years and weathered every storm Alana had ever been caught in. And then some. The US Marines' flag flew high with an American flag beside a satellite dish.

"This is it?" She glanced around. "Is he allowed to live here?"

Locke actually smiled. "Technically, no. But what do you think will happen if Uncle Sam shows up with a police badge to throw a veteran out on his ear and the press gets wind of it?"

"So live and let live, is that it?"

"It's a theory. Brian keeps to himself. He doesn't disturb anyone and asks for the same in return." Locke motioned to a ramshackle shed to the right of the trailer. "He carves animals out of wood and then sells them at a souvenir store at the base of the mountain. And then—" He paused. "What? Wakes up this morning and drives a yakuza soldier to the beach so he can try to kill you?"

He opened his door, but Alana didn't move. "This makes no sense," he said.

She could barely muster up the will to lift her hand. But she couldn't let him know that. "So…why are we interested in this guy, other than that he was the get-away driver from this morning?"

"Maybe he and our knife-man are friends now?" Locke motioned to the file, one leg out of the vehicle. "Brian Wells got out of prison five years ago, moved here. A ten-year stint. Good for us he only dislikes what he calls 'political pawns.' So long as he's taking his medication, we'll be fine."

She grimaced. "Is it bad that I don't want to go in there?"

What if they found another body? She didn't want Locke to see her lose it all over again. It was bad enough he'd seen the aftermath the last time. And why had Brian shown up in her life that morning, if not for a reason that had everything to do with the fact she was a Secret Service agent and he was on their watch list?

His smile softened. "Want to stay here?"

Was he serious? If there was a plot in place, she was going to figure out what it was. Alana stiffened. "No." She shoved the car door open and strode over the soft mossy earth to the front door.

Locke caught up and stretched his arm out in front of her. "Let me."

Who was she to argue? If he wanted to catch the bullet first, that was fine with her. "Be my guest."

He knocked, but no one answered. Locke twisted the door handle and called out as he opened it slowly. This time there was no one inside.

The TV was still on, and a meal in front of the recliner was half-eaten. She'd read in Wells's file he had a blue Chevy truck circa Bill Clinton registered to him. Alana looked around. "This doesn't make sense. Did he just leave in the middle of eating and drive off in his truck?"

Locke wandered to the rear and a sliding door. "You're right. It doesn't make any sense at all."

When Locke ducked into the bedroom—*not going in there, thank you*—she decided to look at the kitchen instead. The sink was full of dishes, and the range top was crusted with charred food. The man needed to crack a window and let in some of that humid hibiscus breeze.

Piled up on the end of the counter was a stack of mail. Magazines. Junk inserts advertising local sales.

A business card.

"Oh, no."

"What is it?" Locke came close enough to look over her shoulder. Didn't he trust her? It was only one text to someone she'd gone to high school with. "Kaylee Preston, Hilo *Explorer* online. Is that—"

"My sister."

"Why does a missing sniper involved in an attempt on your life have your sister's business card?"

FOUR

He watched her blow out a breath. "That is a very good question." Alana unclipped her phone and made a call. After listening for a while, she glanced at the floor. "It's me. Listen, I need to talk to you about something. Can you call me back…please?"

It almost hurt hearing so much longing in the soft alto of her voice. Did he even know what that felt like? Sure, he called his mom on Sundays, but he didn't think he'd ever had that much feeling about someone. Even those closest to him. His sisters were so much older, it wasn't like they'd played together.

Locke walked through the trailer again to give her a minute to gather herself. He stared at the half-eaten meal. Turned off the TV.

No pets. He trailed back to the bedroom. The gun safe in the closet was open, half the racks missing items. Brian had taken at least six weapons—handguns, rifles and a shotgun—assuming no one had looted it since he'd left. Plenty of boxes of shells remained. Clothes spilled out of the drawers, and a green duffel lay crumpled in the corner. With some people, it was hard to tell if they'd been burglarized or if that was just how messy they lived.

Alana said, "Anything?"

Locke glanced around. "He's armed, but he didn't use any of the weapons this morning when I saw him. He just drove."

A loner ex-sniper takes his guns to act as the get-away driver for a yakuza killer? It hardly made sense.

"I called Joe Morton," Alana said. "Get this. He knows this guy, said all the cops do. Apparently he disappears all the time, shows up all over the island drunk and usually raving about political pawns and corruption. All that antigovernment, 'we should live free and not under their thumb' stuff. Joe said they usually take him in for the night and then drive him home the next day." She paused. "I told him you're sure that he's the getaway driver. He's going to update the BOLO to include that information. He said not to worry, they'll find Brian Wells."

Locke motioned to the room around them. "Brian is a drunk, but he's never broken protocol before. Not when he knows the president is coming. He's supposed to be here for this visit, and he's supposed to stay home while the president is in town. That's the arrangement." He shook his head. "Can't put a detail on a man we can't find."

"I know." Alana's look turned dark. "And what's with that half-eaten meal and the TV being on? Did he come back after this morning? The truck is gone, but why walk out in the middle of dinner?"

"We don't have time to look for Brian before the president gets here." Locke motioned to the food, his agent brain spinning with possibilities. "All this could be misdirection, getting us to spin our wheels trying to find him while he's off getting up to no good. He could be plotting something for when the president shows up."

She pressed her lips together.

Locke ran his hand over his head and then squeezed the back of his neck. "We need to reconvene with the team, see if anyone else has had any weird experiences this morning. Something fishy is going on here."

Locke continued, "The only problem is, they don't seem to be connected. There's nothing here that links back to Beatrice's death. He could simply have given the yakuza guy a ride this morning. That could be his only link to this."

Alana turned her phone over and looked at the screen, but it hadn't made a noise. Her sister hadn't returned her call. She clipped her phone back on her belt and went to the couch, where a newspaper had been discarded. "This is dated four days ago. I wonder if he reads it regularly." She glanced around. "I think it would smell more if this meal had been here that long, or there would be animals in here by now."

She worked her mouth side to side as she thought, then flipped the newspaper over. "This has been circled." She brought the paper to him. "It's an ad, a flyer in his paper. There's nothing on the back, but it must have caught his eye. I don't think I even look at these inserts."

"I thought all that stuff was online now," Locke said. "But I guess he doesn't have internet all the way out here, and there's nothing about a cell phone in his file." His eyes scanned the ad. "Cash for work at a gun shop."

"Hang on." Alana tapped the page, the phone number. "That callback number…" She swiped on her phone to a list of numbers. She'd seen that number before.

Today, in fact. "Beatrice's cell phone call logs. That number is on there. She called it, as well."

Alana showed him the notes app on her phone, where she'd transcribed the same number on both the ad and her list. "How's that for a connection."

Locke nodded. "It certainly is one."

"He circled this ad, and Beatrice called that number." She read off the date and time. "Day before yesterday."

Another way Beatrice, Brian Wells and the yakuza member were connected. But her sister as well? She couldn't figure it out.

Locke said, "We don't have time to run down this lead before the president gets here. We already need to get to the team at Hilo airport."

"Get ready to bring the city to a standstill." She sent him a wry smile. "I used to hate when the president came to town. All the roads closed, can't get anywhere, late for everything. Such a pain."

Locke smiled back at her, his look understanding more than amused. "And now we're the ones causing the mayhem."

"At least I'm not trying to get somewhere else, I guess." She shrugged. "So what do we do about this?"

Locke made his way to the front door. They stepped outside, and he scanned the area while Alana shut the trailer door. "Huh."

He turned back. "What is it?"

"This lock is broken. Maybe someone came in and abducted him. Took some guns," she said. "It explains the food he left. And the clothes. Maybe it was after you saw him this morning. He could have returned home, and then it happened?"

Locke shrugged. "Or he had a visitor other than us."

His phone beeped. He read the message aloud. "'Air Force One is four hours out.' Let's get over to Hilo."

She nodded, and they walked to the truck. Alana's phone started to ring, and she whipped it out. Then sighed.

"Not your sister?"

"Nope." She shook her head. "My neighbor in DC. I'll call her back later."

When she was quiet for a while, he apparently decided he needed to get her to talk. Locke said, "So you surfed in competitions, isn't that right?"

She nodded.

"What happened, if you don't mind me asking?" She was sure he knew the story but he must have wanted to hear her tell it.

"Maybe I do mind." In the couple of seconds he took his eyes off the road in front of him, he probably saw the flash of pain in her eyes. She wasn't going to hide it. "What are you doing, Locke? Why the personal question all of a sudden?"

He shrugged one shoulder and flicked his wrist so his watch was straight again. "Just making conversation, getting to know someone I work with better."

"I was so good I was getting approached by swimwear companies, board shops that franchise all the way to New Jersey. Then, bam, I get hit by a swell and my knee kisses the bottom of the ocean while my leg is twisted…" She shook her head. "There was something down there. I still don't know if it was an old board or wreckage from something. All I know is the pain was so bad I wanted them to cut my leg off. I'm pretty sure I screamed at everyone on that beach and cried uncontrollably until they all walked away in embarrassment, even my sister. I was so out of it with pain I don't remember.

"She made sure I knew, though. Told me all about how I screamed in her face to get away from me. I was in the hospital nearly a week, and she didn't come to see me. Then when I got out, she was gone for days, busy studying. When I did see her, she'd barely talk to me." Alana took a breath. "We were never the same after that."

Locke hardly knew what to say. "She didn't know it was the pain talking, not you?"

Alana shrugged.

"And now you're back home?"

"Now I'm back."

Neither of them said much on the drive to the airport, though Locke made a few calls on the car's speakerphone. Alana made notes on her phone for him and sent emails to update their team.

In a break of quiet, her phone rang. "Your neighbor?"

"Nope."

"Your sister?"

"Nope." She answered it. "Mikio Adachi. How are you?" Alana sent Locke a smile as she spoke. They were a good team.

Secret Service work was a team effort, and not just those standing between the president and whatever lone gunman wanted to kill him this week. Their biggest nightmare was a threat that originated with a group. Multiple points of attack, an IED or some other split-second attack that cared nothing for collateral damage.

It was a dangerous world they lived in, and the Secret Service was in the thick of it. Not like frontline soldiers who were shot at every day, but the threat to their lives was very real. Like a police officer who left for work not knowing if today was the day he might not come home.

"Thanks, Mikio. I'll find out what the boss wants to do and get back to you." She hung up. "Okay, so that was interesting. Mikio Adachi was in my graduating class in high school. Everyone knew his dad and his uncle were yakuza. Guess it runs in the family. He said he's the boss now, just volunteered it up like it's no big deal."

"Does he know you're Secret Service?"

"Yes. Though I don't know how." She frowned. "It was like two old friends chatting. I'm not sure why he'd be like that with me. It was a little weird."

The guy probably thought he had a shot at a relationship with her. Like that would make him more powerful, getting a Secret Service agent in his pocket—and his life. "And the yakuza guy we saw at Beatrice's house?"

"That was where things went downhill. Mikio said he couldn't be sure which of his men it was, even though I gave him a pretty good description." She made a face as Locke pulled into the airport and passed through security.

The staff knew Locke's face, so he only had to flash his badge ID and up went the gate. He drove around the building. "Once we look at mug shots and identify the guy, we'll be able to visit this Mikio and get a lot more specific."

"He did say he hadn't heard of anything going on regarding the president's visit. Though he mentioned he had enough problems with his guys. He wasn't surprised we saw one at a murder scene, but he hasn't been all that attentive to whispers circling outside his people."

"So if there is a plot, this guy hasn't heard about it."

"I can talk to him again, find out if there's anyone else on this island worth talking to."

Locke parked beside their other vehicles and pulled the team in for one last briefing. Alana wasn't the only woman on Secret Service protection detail, but he knew she didn't know the other—much older—female agent all that well. He talked them through what had happened and got their reports on every person they had seen. Each pair had emailed him after their visits, but Locke never discounted the personal telling of an experience. He saw things in the inflections and their emotions that he never saw in the body of an email. The two could hardly be compared.

"Okay, you all know where you're supposed to be."

Each team member had a position for the president's arrival. They all hooked up earpieces to their belt radios and checked that communications were working. It was a complicated setup that took all the time from when they arrived at the airport until the plane arrived, and they were each only a piece of the puzzle.

Alana walked beside him as they left the group. "Do you think it's weird no one else on our team had problems with their visits while we found a dead woman and a missing man?"

"Sure, it's weird, but whether it means anything is another matter. There's nothing we can do about it this minute. We run the president's arrival just like we do everything else. By the book. Stick to what you know. Remember your training, and if something happens, we'll all deal with it. All of us, together."

Alana nodded.

"When you get a minute later on, call Officer Morton. Find out if the cops discovered what that call in Beatrice's history relates to. Maybe they'll know whose number it is, because I certainly don't believe she's answering an ad for work at a gun shop like Brian Wells. It's a solid link between them, and the police have the jurisdiction to look it up. If we prove there's a link, then it'll help us when they find Brian Wells."

"Okay, I can do that." She looked relieved, probably because he hadn't asked her to call Ray.

"And don't worry. We'll get to the bottom of it."

They walked toward the tarmac as the plane came into view. The sleek lines of Air Force One gleamed in the setting sun as the plane's brakes engaged and the president's aircraft descended to the tarmac. It was a textbook landing, the arrival of the president signaling Locke's team's switch from preparation to action as they aided in guarding POTUS on his vacation.

Locke prayed as the plane slowed to a stop. For the whole trip, for all the personnel, for his team. He prayed for their investigation into Beatrice's murder, and for the missing marine—that he wasn't hurt or planning to hurt anyone.

Locke keyed his radio. "Air Force One is on the ground."

FIVE

Alana stood beside Locke while the president descended from the plane. The entourage—which included the governor of Hawaii, a number of her staff members and local FBI agents—each took their turns shaking hands with the president. He'd been traveling all day, but his suit wasn't rumpled and his gray hair looked freshly cut. The barber was probably on the plane.

Locke was at attention, like some military sentry guarding his liege lord. Alana didn't quite know how to pull that off, but she'd probably have to learn it.

As the president made his way down the line, he made small talk with the governor, who nearly tripped over her feet just to keep up with the man's athletic stride.

Sweat beaded on Alana's forehead. The temperature had risen as they'd waited for the plane to land and then taxi its way over to them. She glanced around, knowing exactly where each Secret Service agent was located. It was a reflex, assessing the area for danger even though every position was covered.

When she'd least suspected it, that hand had reached up and grabbed for her foot. Her abdomen still stung—she should have brought her painkillers with her, or taken some before they got out of the car. But then Locke would have seen it, and he'd have known she was hurting.

The first lady descended from the plane hand in hand with their twelve-year-old son. The boy was one of Alana's favorite people. Their paper airplane competition had been running for three months now, but she hadn't decided if his using paper with embossed lettering on the top that he'd retrieved from his father's desk gave him an unfair advantage. Her origami paper was lighter, but those gold letters weighted down the rear of his plane.

Locke tapped the side of her arm. Did he think she wasn't paying attention? Alana didn't have time to glare at him before the president stopped alongside Locke.

"Director Locke."

"Sir. Did you have a good trip?"

"Yes, thank you." It wasn't just rote conversation. Alana knew what people on TV said about the president, but she saw genuine care in his eyes. He appreciated people—the way some presidents never did—and this president always took a moment to greet them. It made guarding him so much more enjoyable.

Locke said, "If you have time, I'd like a minute. I have some things I'd like to run past you."

The president nodded. "I'll have that added to my calendar. Perhaps later?" He glanced at an aide behind him, who made a notation on a tablet with a stylus pen. The president glanced at Alana, his blue eyes smiling with concern. "Are you feeling okay after this morning, Agent Preston?"

He knew about the attack? "Yes, sir. I'm good, thank you for asking." What had he been told? She didn't like the idea that he might not think she was up to the task of protecting him when it was just a cut on her stomach and a couple of bruises. Okay, so she'd stopped breathing for a minute, but that was just her body's way of protecting itself from swallowing more water. She was fine now. Didn't she look fine?

"Good to hear." He motioned to Locke. "Stick with the director, he'll look out for you." Alana nodded. What else could she do? He thought she needed Locke to look after her.

Locke said, "That's actually what I wanted to speak with you about, sir."

The governor of Hawaii broke off what she'd been saying to the person beside her and glanced at Locke and Alana, like *Why are these people important?* Alana resisted the temptation to smirk. That just wouldn't be professional, and neither would accidentally tripping the woman like she was imagining. Not that Alana had a vindictive streak, she just had a serious problem with anyone who considered others beneath them.

The president nodded in reply to Locke's statement. "Director Matthews filled me in on everything that happened today on the way here." He glanced to her, including her in his statement. "I can't believe some random beach bum would try to hurt you, Agent Preston."

Alana couldn't answer. She was stunned, but was it Matthews who'd told the president it was random, or was that the conclusion the president had drawn himself?

Locke said, "Sir—"

"Make that appointment with my aide, James." The president motioned to the governor to continue on and gave Alana a compassionate smile as he moved away.

The aide paused long enough to say, "Seven thirty tomorrow morning."

Locke didn't look happy, but he nodded anyway. She knew he liked his morning routine, whether they were in the White House or Hawaii or anywhere else in the world. She'd seen him with his coffee, reading his Bible. Fact was, he probably just didn't want to wait until tomorrow, and Alana wasn't that happy about it, either.

Director William Matthews strode over, wearing sunglasses and the same earpiece with the clear coiled wire they all wore with their suits. The older man's hair was silver and shined as brightly as his shoes. His tie was red because it was Thursday—Alana had figured that out after the first month.

"Let's go, Patricia." William nodded toward the president. The aide turned and scurried along beside him.

Alana glanced around again. Why did it feel like she was being watched? Likely there were multiple sets of eyes on her—Secret Service, local police and residents there to spot the president. Now that he'd moved through the area, they could take a break. The team who traveled with the president were tasked with his protection and kept a short distance from him. Director Matthews brought up the rear with the aide, Patricia.

Alana hung back with Locke, the rest of their team around them. Nothing to do for the rest of the evening but field phone calls and man the office they'd created in a hotel conference room. She sighed. This was the team she was on, and if she wanted to get out of the rookie seat, she had to prove she was a team player. Too bad surfing was usually only a one-person sport.

"Okay?"

His question jerked her from her thoughts. Alana

pasted on a smile. "Fine." The sweat hadn't let up. Her palms were sticky. What was wrong with her? She glanced around again. *Staring.* Locke's attention was on her, but there was something else.

"You're not fine."

Alana kept her gaze moving. "Someone…"

"You feel it, too. I thought it was just the president's arrival, but maybe it's something else." He shifted closer to her. "Your instincts may very well be spot-on. Tell me what you're feeling."

"Like I'm being watched." She shook her head. "I mean, *we* are being watched."

"You said *I*, and that's fine. It might be important. Someone targeted you this morning. Tried to kill you. Your instinct is telling you it's you that's in danger, not us in general as Secret Service agents. That instinct isn't a bad thing."

She heard the edge in his voice, but he didn't look at her. Logically she knew he cared. Probably because if she was killed it would be a pain to fill out all those incident reports and then find someone to replace her. Fine, he'd probably cry at her funeral. Or at least get a little teary. Afterward he'd go back to work, though. That was Locke.

"Alana? Someone tried to kill you, remember?"

"You think I forgot?" Alana turned. Too late she realized she'd twisted her torso without moving her hips and shoulders at the same time. Pain sliced through her middle, and she groaned.

"Easy," Locke said.

Alana hung her head, hands on her abdomen as she sucked in the fresh air of home. They needed to follow up with the cops, find out how her sister could be linked to the sniper and why a yakuza soldier had tried to kill her this morning. She had a whole lot of questions, and while getting answers wouldn't make her stomach stop hurting, it would help them get to the bottom of this.

"She okay?" one of the team asked.

Locke set his hand on Alana's shoulder. "She will be." He gave it a squeeze. "Let's go, Preston."

Time to suck it up. Alana straightened. "I'm good." Her stomach flipped over. She took a step, and her knees buckled.

Locke grabbed her elbow. "Let's get you to the car, and then we'll get some food in you."

Alana nodded. "I know a place. It's not far from here."

"It's right here."

"The restaurant?" Locke slowed the car to a crawl past the fourplex in a complex of buildings that were all exactly the same. Still, these looked like they were on the higher end of the rental spectrum. The cars outside were nicer, but that was hardly a gauge of upward mobility. So many low-rent, low-income neighborhoods had parking lots full of brand-new cars.

He pulled up to the curb and put the SUV in Park.

"That's my sister's place." Alana motioned to one of the units, all lit by street lights. "Upstairs, left side. Lights are out, so she probably isn't home. The car that's registered to her isn't here."

"Any reason why you couldn't just tell me we were going to stop by your sister's on the way to eat?" He wanted to say more, but the woman was seriously flagging. She'd deflated onto the seat, and though she'd thought he wasn't watching, he'd seen her take pain-killers. Why did she feel the need to hide it?

Alana's attention didn't leave her sister's apartment. Locke said, "Do you want to go knock on the door?"

She bristled. "No, I'm sure she's not there."

"Did you try to call her again?"

"Sure. A couple of times." Alana's face gave nothing away.

"I know you're not close." He didn't know what else to say. "I could go knock on the door, if you want."

"No!" She didn't even hesitate.

"Okay." Locke studied her. Maybe this was all because she'd had a long, rough day. They both needed rest—but they needed food first. "So is there a restaurant?"

Alana told him where it was. Locke entered it on the GPS, which came up with the name. Not a chain restaurant—this seemed more like a hole-in-the-wall diner. "Is this place good?"

Her eyebrows shot up. "Of course it's good, and the coffee is thick enough it'll put hairs on your chest."

There was no way he was going to let that throw-away comment go by. "Because I…"

A tiny smile played at her lips. "It's a dumb expression, but you know what I mean."

"Yeah, I know what you mean."

He drove to the restaurant, aware of her attention on him in his peripheral vision. When they pulled into a space outside, he said, "Okay, do I have mustard on my face or what?"

"Sorry." She shifted in her seat. "You just seem…I don't know, relaxed?"

"As opposed to uptight?"

"Locke—"

"It's fine. I know what everyone says about me." Uptight was the least of it, so he didn't blame her for being weirded out. He had let his guard down since they left the airport. The harder part of their trip was over, but something had changed between them today.

"I shouldn't have made it obvious."

Locke shook his head. "It's okay, Alana." Her face softened at his use of her name. "It's been a long day, and no one can keep their guard up forever." Though he could see her still hanging on for dear life to her solid plan of proving herself, sooner or later she was going to have to admit that getting attacked that morning had rocked her.

He'd thought she would do it at the airport, when she'd nearly collapsed. But she'd soldiered on. Locke admired her tenacity. Alana was determined to get everyone to see her as a capable Secret Service agent. But she also needed to know when to accept help. She wasn't a one-woman task force—they had to be able to rely on each other, and not just as a backup plan.

But this wasn't about work. Today had changed *them*. He'd pulled her out of the ocean bleeding and not breathing. Locke had chased her attacker from the scene and then from Beatrice's house after he'd successfully murdered the old lady.

Locke had been bested, and Alana had been hurt, and there was nothing he could do to change either of those facts. What he could do was make sure it never happened again. And that started with both of them being on their game.

He grabbed the door handle. "Food, coffee. Sleep. The cops are searching for Brian Wells and his yakuza associate. Tomorrow we'll figure all this out. Sound good?"

Alana nodded. She got out first, so Locke brought up the rear just because deliberately passing her would be too awkward. Cars drove past, and music poured from a bar two doors down. People talking, laughing—the night crowd had come out.

The windows of the restaurant were wide, and the orange light from within illuminated the busy tables. Nearly every one of them was occupied by someone, most by two or three people. A couple of families. Half a dozen of the patrons were uniformed police, and Locke figured at least three of the men eating in plain clothes were detectives or off-duty officers.

Alana reached the door. He caught her gaze and said, "This is a cop restaurant."

She didn't rub in the fact she'd surprised him, but neither did she react like this might be a ruse and she was mad he'd figured it out.

Locke said, "We're not here to eat, are we? Or we're not here *just* to eat, at least." Was she going to take a break ever?

Alana didn't answer; she simply wandered inside. A red dot on the door frame caught his eye. As quickly as he saw it, it disappeared. Had it been his imagination? Locke glanced around at businesses across the street. Rooftops. Hair pricked on the back of his neck, but no lone gunman sat waiting for his moment. Locke shook off the feeling and followed her in. Probably he hadn't seen anything, and he was just amped up, riding on adrenaline from the crazy day they'd had.

Alana spoke with a couple of uniformed officers and then sat on a stool at the counter. Locke wandered over just as the waitress flipped two mugs upright and filled them with thick black coffee. He was going to be awake all night if he finished that.

The waitress tossed menus on the counter. Locke said, "Thanks," but she'd already moved away. He glanced at Alana.

She gripped her menu and stared at it with her eyebrows raised. "So, the president calls you James, does he?"

"Only when he feels he needs to chastise me."

"If it pleases your honor, let the record state that I didn't even know that was your name."

Locke laughed and she glanced at him, a gleam of humor in her eyes. He said, "So noted."

"James Locke."

Boy, he liked the way that rolled off her tongue. So he used his spy-enchanting-a-lady voice and said, "Alana Preston."

It was her turn to laugh. She cleared her throat, and Locke spotted the smallest of blushes pinking her cheeks. He looked at his menu to try to diffuse some of whatever this was between them. He had to brush it off, or she'd know it was a thing. It wouldn't help them if they lost focus and drifted off the map into feelings territory instead of spending their time figuring out why someone had tried to kill her that morning, and what it had to do with her sister.

Alana couldn't know he cared about her enough that seeing her get hurt had rocked him. His reaction had torn down a wall—surprising him as much as it seemed to surprise her. She couldn't know it was because he was attracted to her. That wasn't going to help him keep the president safe.

Locke looked up from his menu. Next to the opening to the kitchen where plates were being delivered to the waitress, was a wall of framed photos.

"Four down, three across."

Locke counted frames. Four down, three across was a picture with an '80s feel to it—two men in suits and a little girl. Dark hair down to her waist, the girl smiled wide as she leaned against one of the men. "Is that…"

"That's me. Kaylee had dance class, so we came in for pie before we had to go pick her up. She was so mad she never got on the wall."

Locke set his menu down. The waitress made her way back over and refilled Alana's already empty coffee. He'd barely touched his.

"What can I get ya?"

Alana said, "I'll take a—"

The front window smashed. *Bang.*

Bang.

Bullets flew, the sound of shots like fireworks popping. Between each was a split second of deathly silence. No one moved, every patron too shocked to speak.

Bang. Someone screamed.

Locke pushed off the rungs of the stool, slammed into Alana, and they hit the floor with him covering her.

SIX

Locke's elbow smarted. His ears rang over the distant sound of men yelling. Cops sprang into action as drywall dust settled around them, and Locke rubbed the grit from his eyes. Alana lay beside him on the tile floor, her eyes shut for the second time that day. He hated doing it, but Locke pressed his fingers against her neck.

When he felt her pulse thump under his fingertips, Locke swiped them across her jaw. She looked so much younger, and all those protective feelings he'd discovered that morning swelled to life again. He was not going to let her die.

Alana's eyes flew open, and she sucked in a breath.

"Easy." Locke looked her over. There was no blood, as neither of them had been injured, but the spots of red on her shirt—over where she'd been cut that morning—weren't good. The wound was bleeding again. "Don't move until I get someone to come look at you."

An officer—Joe Morton from that morning—crouched by them. "You guys okay?"

Locke nodded.

"I'm good." Alana started to get up.

"Easy," Joe said. "Maybe you should stay there until we can get you checked out."

She shook her head. "Save it for someone who really needs it."

Locke supported her as she sat up. If she'd tried to stand, he'd have pulled rank and made her stay sitting, but thankfully he didn't have to.

Joe got up and walked away, and Locke surveyed the room. The ringing in his ears had stopped. Bullet holes peppered the walls. One man was down—a plainclothes cop, badge on his hip—and two EMTs were there already. Across the room a uniformed officer helped another to his feet, blood running from a nasty gash on his temple. It was a lot of carnage for a sniper. A wide smattering of bullet holes and no one dead yet—though the EMTs were scrambling. They lifted the man and raced out with a handful of officers surrounding them.

Had this been a targeted attack and all this was simply collateral? If the shooter had been aiming for Alana, he hadn't done a good job. In fact, shooting up a busy restaurant was a really bad way to try to kill Alana. If this was their sniper, Brian Wells, he was either rusty or just trying to send a message to them.

Alana hissed and touched her abdomen. "That smarts."

"We should have a doctor look at it."

She waved off his concern with her other hand. "I'll be fine, I just jarred it when you landed on me."

"Sorry for saving your life."

She pressed her lips together. "That's not what I meant." Still, tears filled her eyes.

"Hey." Locke touched her cheek.

Alana looked at him like he'd grown two heads. "You're softening the blow. You're going to report all of this, and it's going to go in my file that you saved me and I didn't even do anything."

"Of course I'm going to write a report," he said. "But what does it matter that I moved first?"

"Because I didn't do anything. I didn't react fast enough." The tears gathered and threatened to spill over. She touched her stomach again and winced.

"It isn't a competition. Of course I was faster," he said. "Do you know how long I've been a Secret Service agent?" When she didn't answer, he continued, "At this point I just about flatten my nephew on the driveway when the fireworks go off on the Fourth of July. It's a reflex, and I do it without thinking. I'm just worried I hurt you. I'm pretty heavy."

"But why didn't I grab you and dive? What's wrong with me?"

"Alana—"

"No, I want to know. I've had the same training as you. Why didn't I dive to the floor? I didn't even react."

She really thought that was a problem? After the day they'd had? "You were injured this morning, and we've been on since then. Don't be so hard on yourself."

Alana shook her head.

He didn't let her argue. "No, listen to me. This isn't a training exercise. Nothing that happened today is anything you were prepared for. You reacted perfectly adequately."

"I don't want adequate." She lifted her gaze. "I want to be as good as you."

"You will be." His heart warmed with the thought that she'd aspire to be like him, but Locke wasn't anything special. "In time, you will be. But right now you need to give yourself a break. You need rest."

"You're going to write this up, and I'll look bad."

"No, you'll look human."

"That's not—"

Locke's phone rang. He ignored it, and the fact she'd probably been about to say that it wasn't acceptable that she was human. What else did she expect?

He raised up to a crouch and held out his hands. "Let's get you to a chair. When we're done with the police, we can go back to the hotel and sleep."

Alana pressed her lips together and said nothing while he helped her to a chair. Locke took a moment to pray for her. She needed peace—anyone would, after the day they'd had. His heart reached for her, but he had to pull back. Touching her, even if it was only on her cheek again, would be a bad idea.

Alana probably didn't feel anything in return. She had freaked out when he'd touched her face. Probably she'd been too thrown to tell him to back off, or that she wasn't interested. She'd had a hard day, so he wasn't going to blame her for that. But he couldn't help thinking she probably didn't want that from him.

Locke wasn't after a relationship. They had to keep things professional on the job. But still, it would have been nice to get a different reaction than that "What on earth are you doing?" look. She seemed to only think about work. Sure, she was trying to shake off that rookie label, but she was pushing herself entirely too hard. One of these days she was going to burn out from the stress and exertion of going after perfection so hard.

She kind of reminded him of…him.

At least the way everyone else saw him. But Locke knew how to manage that drive to be the best. And when he didn't measure up, he didn't beat himself up. He simply thanked God he was capable of everything he *had* done and didn't worry about what was impossible. He'd learned his limits, and beyond them was the ability to live through another colleague getting hurt.

That was why he'd dived first.

"Do you think this was Brian Wells?"

Locke pulled up a chair and sat in front of her. "It could have been."

"But was he trying to kill me? He could have killed everyone in this room, or he could have waited until we walked out and used one bullet."

"Exactly. We don't know why he chose to do this, but it's undeniable that he wanted to cause a considerable amount of carnage. And unless we find him, he could hurt even more people."

Alana clenched her fists on her lap so that her knuckles went white. "We have to find him."

"The cops have a BOLO out. As soon as they get a call, they'll let us know and we'll go with them to pick him up."

She nodded. "Good."

"Are you okay?" She still looked a little pale, shaken up but not nearly like she had this morning. "You look better than you did earlier."

"Good." She lifted her chin.

Not this again. Locke didn't need more of her pretending she wasn't hurt just so he'd be impressed. "I mean better than when you weren't breathing."

She grimaced. "Great. At least I'm alive, is that it?"

"It is a plus." Locke wasn't doing very well if she didn't get he was just trying to help her feel better. She wasn't up to responding to his humor, or she was misunderstanding him on purpose because she didn't want to talk about it.

His phone rang again. Locke glanced at the screen. "It's William."

"You should get it."

He nodded. "I'll fill him in on what happened."

"Tell him I'm fine."

Locke didn't respond to that, he just swiped to answer the call and stepped away.

Alana waited until his back was turned and let out her breath. She slumped lower in the chair and touched her stomach. It hurt really badly. So badly it was hard to keep from Locke exactly how much it hurt. The sting was going to keep her awake all night. Still, there was work to do.

Alana braced her hand on the table and pushed herself to stand just in time to see her brother walk in the door. Great. All she needed was another overbearing male with that dark "I should have protected you" look on his face.

"Sit down." Ray stalked toward her. "You aren't fooling anyone."

Alana slumped back into the chair.

Ray stood over her, not in uniform like he had been earlier.

"Were you off duty?"

His expression didn't change.

"Are you mad at me?" What had she done to warrant that?

Ray perched on the edge of the table and looked down at her. "I'm not mad, Alana. I'm worried about you. Yes, I was off duty, but I got called in, and not just because everyone knows you were attacked in the water this morning."

"I'm—"

"Fine. Yeah, I know." His dark eyebrows pinched together. He had the tan she used to have when she lived here. Ray had always been into surfing, running, kayaking. They'd spent hours together at the beach with Kaylee, and Ray had taken both Alana and her sister surfing their first time.

He was the one who'd encouraged her to enter competitions. He'd been her number-one supporter and had been as devastated as Alana was when she got injured. She hadn't spoken to him for days afterward, and he'd never visited her in the hospital. When she got home things had been awkward, and in the years since not much had changed.

She mostly figured that devastation, coupled with his feeling sorry for her—or guilty he'd pushed her into surfing—meant he hadn't been able to face her. And they'd never figured out how to get past the death of what they both thought the future would bring.

Alana was done with it. "Why are you giving me a hard time? I'm only trying to do my job. A job, I'll remind you, that you told me to go and do."

"Because you decided to go to the mainland and try for the Secret Service."

"You told me to do it! You told me not to be a cop and said I had to be better than that."

He'd actually told her to be better than him, which she still didn't understand. Their father had insisted over and over that she was destined for great things. After she got hurt and had to let her surfing dreams die, her father still told her that same thing.

Now it was up to her to go find those great things, because they weren't going to happen to her sitting at home. She was doing something great, something important. So why did she feel so inadequate?

Ray stared at her like he could read her thoughts. "Because you are better than that, Alana. You're better than me, than Dad." He waved at the room. "Than *this*."

"Why?" It made no sense. "I'm not better than you. That's crazy." She didn't want to think bad of her father, but why tell one child they were better than the others? It made it worse that Ray believed him.

"Just because you don't see it doesn't make it untrue."

Alana got up. She moved past her brother, but he caught her elbow. "That isn't what I came here to talk about."

Alana shrugged one shoulder. She would hear him out, but she wasn't going to wait around all night to do it. "Make it fast." He didn't need to know she had to go because she was about to collapse.

"It's about Kaylee."

Great. Another person Alana didn't understand. "Do you know why her business card was at Brian Wells's house?"

"That's not what I want to talk about, either. But if I had to guess, it'd be about a story. Everything with Kaylee is about work. Like someone else I know."

"Ray, I need to figure out who keeps trying to kill me and whether Kaylee is connected to it."

Ray shrugged. "That isn't our biggest problem."

"They tried to *kill me*."

"I know." Ray ran one hand over his hair, a familiar move that strung a pang in her. "But I'm looking for Kaylee, too. I can't find her."

"She's missing?" When he nodded, Alana said, "Is she connected to this?" She couldn't believe Kaylee could be a party to people trying to kill Alana. Her sister couldn't hate her that much.

Ray said, "Kaylee is connected to Mikio Adachi."

"How?"

"How do you think?"

They were in a relationship. What else would it be? "That doesn't help, you know. It only makes things more complicated."

"We'll figure it out."

"We?" Now he wanted there to be a connection between them? "If Kaylee seriously is romantically involved with the head of the Japanese mafia, what's to figure out? You should have stopped her. You shouldn't have let her do this." It probably put his career in jeopardy, his sister being linked to the yakuza. Secret Service intelligence probably knew that about her, while Alana hadn't. Kaylee's choices put them all at risk. "You shouldn't have let her do this to *you*."

"I don't get you, Alana. In one breath you don't want to work with me, and in the next you're freaking out because you care about my life." He shook his head. "I don't understand."

"Well, that makes two of us, Ray." She folded her arms. "Why didn't you stop it?"

"Maybe because Kaylee won't speak to me. We've been drifting apart for a while, and she hasn't answered my calls for months. She's been mad at me since you left because she thinks I let you go."

"She wanted me to get out of her life. You didn't tell her that you *told* me to go as well?"

"Going to the mainland was your decision."

Alana pressed her lips together. She wasn't even going to go there. "It's not like she'll listen to me."

"She told me once she couldn't believe you actually went."

Alana glanced away. Locke was still on his phone,

but his eyes were on her. His gaze flicked to Ray, and she saw a question there. Alana shook her head. She didn't need another well-meaning man messing up her life. She had enough of that already. Locke was supposed to think she was a strong, capable agent. Not a woman with a disastrous home life that was currently encroaching on business and making it incredibly difficult to do her job without crying. Why couldn't things just be good? Why did her life have to be so *hard*?

She looked away from Locke before almost crying became actually doing it. Again. She sucked in a breath and faced her brother. "So we have no idea where Mikio, Kaylee, the man who tried to kill me or Brian Wells are. Do you have anything that will actually help me?"

"Alana—"

"No, you don't get to be nice now because you were a jerk a decade ago. Because I know you, and you'd sooner swallow your boot than actually ask a person for forgiveness." She wasn't going to give it to him until he told her he was sorry for real. Not just this guilt-laden niceness. It was infuriating.

Locke strode over. "Alana?"

He wasn't calling her Preston in front of her brother? That was a first. She didn't have the energy to respond, though, even if it did feel nice.

"One more thing, and then back to the hotel."

Ray said, "What is it?" Did he think he was part of this? Alana shot him a glare and then looked at Locke.

"There's been a sighting of Brian Wells."

SEVEN

Locke found her at the coffee station that had been set up in the corner of the conference room they were using for briefings. Alana poured two packets of sugar into her paper cup, then grabbed a spoon. Last night's sniper sighting had been a bust, and they still got back to the hotel in the middle of the night. Apparently she was a sugar-and-cream-with-a bit-of-coffee person. He smiled at her. "You like it sweet."

With her eyes on him, Alana reached for her cup, hit the edge with the plastic spoon and dumped the whole thing over. "Oh, no!"

Locke grabbed a stack of napkins and helped her mop up the mess. Alana's cheeks pinked. He said, "Sorry I made you spill."

She shook her head, her hands jittery. "Don't worry about it." She took the mess of coffee-soaked napkins from him and dumped them in the trash. Locke poured two cups of coffee and handed the one with milk and sugar to her. She glanced at his black cup and wrinkled her nose.

"You should try it sometime."

Alana shook her head. "Super-sweet coffee is my indulgence."

"Did you sleep okay?" She looked far more rested but wasn't moving like she was up to extreme exertion.

Alana shrugged. "No one tried to drown me, stab me or shoot me, so that was good."

"Right." She'd had nightmares, though. He was sure of it. "Give it time. You don't have to bounce back straight away." They'd had one of the hardest days in months yesterday—and with their schedules, that was saying something.

"I'm fine, Locke." She turned and wandered to her seat.

There was an empty one beside her, but Locke moved to the front. He'd rather sit with her at their morning briefing, if everyone wouldn't have taken it as a sign they were becoming friends...which often led to more. They worked in close quarters, and things happened. People gave in to their feelings and fell in love. It was why Locke had to keep that professional distance.

It wasn't against the rules for Secret Service agents to have a relationship, but they worked long hours and were reassigned every three years. It was hardly a recipe for marital bliss.

William Matthews swept into the room. "Good morning, everyone. Thank you for coming." He set his iPad on the podium up front.

The hotel had set aside an entire wing for their offices, along with several floors surrounding the president's suite. It was easy to assume the president was in more danger those times they were on foreign soil where the situation was harder to contain, but the real danger was close-quarters attacks at home. Infiltration. An incendiary device planted in a hotel.

They could sweep cars, cordon off areas, clear roads and hotel rooms, do the best they could to eliminate the possibilities. But the fact was it would never be completely secure.

This president wasn't known for breaking formation just to shake hands, as some were. He held to the boundaries they gave him and offered respect to the agents assigned to take a bullet if necessary. Locke wasn't required to like him, but it helped that the man was easy to admire.

"Top of the agenda for today is the president's ribbon cutting at the new wing of the University of Hawaii. He'll be making a speech." William listed off agents on his team and several from Locke's and gave them detail assignments. "POTUS has also decided he wants to attend the surf invitational Saturday morning at the Hapuna Beach State Recreation Area. Locke—" he glanced over, probably to make sure he had Locke's attention "—you're the lead on the surf competition."

Locke gritted his molars and nodded. The president had to have told William yesterday, so why was this the first Locke was hearing about it? Locke's morning coffee with the president had been cancelled so the Commander in Chief could rest, but he could have been informed of this by email.

The surf invitational had been on the list of possible events the president might want to attend, so it wasn't completely out of the blue. But why announce it in the briefing when Locke always gave William a heads-up beforehand so he could prepare? During the briefing was the time to announce to their teams who was working on what.

Alana sat up straighter. "The invitational is at Hapuna Bay?"

Locke shifted in his seat. William looked at his iPad, then said, "That's the information I have. Is there a problem?"

Alana's brow crinkled. "No, it's fine. There are just better spots to surf than Hapuna. Though I guess it's good for a public competition, and there are plenty of access and exit points, so it won't be as hard as it could be for us to extract the president if we need to." She paused. "It's just not the best *surf* spot on the island, but those are all secret anyway."

"We're talking about the safety of the president of the United States, Ms. Preston, not the best 'surf' spots." William lifted his fingers to make quote marks. "How about we focus on our job?"

Alana nodded, then lifted her coffee and sipped. She covered it well, but she'd been chastised. Locke would have said the same thing, though he'd have worded it differently. He knew Alana now. He knew what she looked like with tears in her eyes, and the brave face she showed the world even when she was in pain. He'd probably have swallowed the comment and let her statement go. William didn't need to be a jerk just because he was jet-lagged and had a long day ahead of him.

"Alana and I will head over to Hapuna and coordinate for Saturday."

William's gaze flickered with something Locke didn't understand. Maybe William was just tired from yesterday's travel day. Yes, if something happened today and Alana and Locke were on the detail protecting the president, it put POTUS at risk.

He understood why William had put them on the surf competition. It was Director Matthews's job on this trip to hand out assignments. Locke and Alana needed a day that was essentially admin, while the rest of his team was swallowed into William's and put on protection detail.

Locke would have done the same thing if he was heading up the protection detail on this trip. His team was the advance team, and he and Alana had been involved in a couple of "incidents" the day before, so it made sense for it to happen this way. But that didn't mean he had to like it, and it seemed Alana didn't much, either.

Still, she was injured. An easier day would do them both good.

The rest of their team dispersed with William and his team. Locke checked in with each, as he liked to keep his finger on the pulse of how they were doing. Mostly they were just concerned about Alana, so he reassured them he'd take care of her.

He'd spoken to Ray late last night, having gotten Alana's brother's number from one of the other officers at the restaurant. Ray promised to stay on top of the search for the yakuza man who had nearly killed Alana in the ocean.

The hunt for Beatrice's killer took precedence with the local police, as it had been a bigger incident, but Ray was looking into the knife attack on Alana personally and everyone was searching for the sniper.

Locke didn't doubt that Ray cared about his sister. They shared a common worry for her safety. So Locke would protect her, and Ray would let him know any information he learned.

Alana would be safe, and Locke would help her stay that way while they did their jobs here.

Alana was headed for the door.

"Whoa, Preston. Slow down."

She glanced back. "I need to catch William. I want to be assigned to the president's detail, not sidelined on coordinating the surf competition. I don't think he knows I'm fine." She frowned at him, but kept walking. "Did you tell him I'm not fine, is that why you want me on this with you?"

She wasn't, but still. "I didn't say anything. He probably pieced it together."

"Well, then there's no reason he couldn't have reassigned me."

The elevator had already left. Alana jabbed at the button.

"Hold up a second."

She set her hands on her hips and glanced at him. Not mad, but close to it.

Locke said, "We're headed to the surf competition. That's our job for today." Her job: feeling useful. His job: keeping her safe. Their job together: to be Secret Service agents who protected the president.

Alana didn't pout exactly—that wasn't what people like them did. But if she'd been anyone else, she likely would have. "I don't want to be sidelined."

"That isn't what's happening." He stepped closer. "And it won't reflect well if you argue with William."

Alana sighed. "I still don't like it."

"How's your…" He motioned to where she'd been cut the day before.

"It aches, but it's okay."

Locke said, "Years ago, if you were injured so you couldn't go surfing, what would you have done instead?"

"Sat on the beach and watched. Cleaned my board. Helped the others if they needed pointers."

"Those things are important. They're not just busy work to pass the time. And that's what this is." He tugged on her arm. "So give yourself a break, okay?"

The elevator doors opened. Alana strode into the empty car, and he followed her. She pressed the button for the lobby and then turned to him. "Taking a break doesn't make you a winner."

She was still mad when they pulled into the parking lot at Hapuna. Memories washed over her as she looked around. The sound of the surf was a balm to her restless spirit. She ached to surf, but that would have to wait a few days—though she figured if she had to, she could push it to a couple of days at the most. It would sting, but she could do it.

Alana still wanted to go back and talk to William. He didn't need to sideline her with Locke, she could pass any physical test he threw at her—so long as he didn't ask her to surf. But yeah, she knew why he wanted her with Locke, separated from the rest of the team. And the president. If someone tried to kill her again, they could hit the president by accident. Alana would never forgive herself if something happened to the president and it was her fault. Not a good career move. Unless being beside the president was the one place she might be safe—if Brian Wells, their missing sniper, didn't *want* to kill him, just her. Threatening the president was a whole different ball game than killing her. One a lot of people would think twice about.

Locke was looking at his iPad again, on the website for the surf invitational.

"There's nothing on there that I can't tell you," she said. "Plus, you know these things are like sixty percent word of mouth. The website is for tourists and corporations. Sponsors and such."

"Okay, so tell me about it."

"First I have a question." She unbuckled her seat belt and got her gun from the glove box. "Do you think Brian Wells wants to kill the president? Maybe this yakuza man and the missing sniper who seem to be targeting me are actually plotting to assassinate POTUS."

"It's possible, but I think unlikely until we get proof it's a plot. Right now we have to go on what we know." Locke got his weapon and climbed out of the SUV, iPad in hand.

He'd make notes, and they would decide which plan to protect the president they would enact for the invitational. Their scenarios fit every circumstance, but they were based on half a dozen prearranged plans and then tweaked for the variables of location, crowd size and expected threat level. Not as exciting as developing a scenario from scratch, but it meant the teams could work within an established framework and there wasn't the lag where they each had to figure out how their part fit with the rest of the agents.

Alana checked the time on her cell phone. "The coordinator should be here in a minute. The admin assistant I spoke to said eight forty-five."

Locke nodded.

"The surf isn't bad this morning. If the weather holds

out hopefully it'll be good for Saturday." Surfing in the rain was miserable but arguably kind of fun, since it made the waves look bigger than they really were.

Locke didn't say anything. When she glanced at him, Alana saw that he scanned the whole area. His eyes were alert, his whole body tense like he was ready for the world around them to erupt.

"Locke."

"Preston."

Great. They were back to business. Alana wanted to roll her eyes. "Guess it's time to sunbathe and get a shave ice."

"Yep." The word was low, like his thoughts were somewhere else.

She walked off. If he wasn't going to listen to her, then she wasn't going to stick around. She could protect herself.

The morning surfers returned her wave. Alana walked the beach until sand gravitated into her shoes, and then she pulled them off and strolled with them dangling from her fingers. She checked the time on her phone and then circled back toward the parking lot. Locke stood at the edge of the sand, his shoes still on. Hands on his hips.

When she got close, he said, "Feel better now?"

"Actually, yes." The beach had always been a balm.

"For the record," Locke said, "I would not be opposed to trying a shave ice."

She didn't have time to answer. Or to process the fact he'd evidently never had one before. A van door shut, and Alana saw a familiar face. That was the coordinator for the surf invitational? Of course. She grinned at the man as he approached in board shorts and a threadbare vest, no shoes. His big belly hung over the tied string on his shorts.

"Alana Preston!" Ikamu ran the last few steps, his big frame barreling toward her like a freight train.

Locke braced, but Alana brushed past him. This was going to hurt, but she didn't care. She grinned at her friend. "Ikamu!" He hauled her off the ground and she squealed as the big man hugged her. Her stomach smarted, but not too much.

"We're supposed to be meeting the surf coordinator, not socializing with old friends."

Alana grinned. "Ikamu taught me how to surf like a pro. So, yes, I'm socializing with an old friend, but he's also in charge of the invitational." She glanced at Ikamu, who nodded. "The president wants to come."

"For reals?"

She nodded. "There's a lot to prepare, but with your help we can get it ironed out."

"Sounds good, sista. I knew inviting his niece to compete would be a good idea. She's real good. Nearly as good as you." He bumped her shoulder with his football-size one. "But I didn't think the big man would come. You think he's gonna wear shorts?"

Alana grinned. "That would be fun to see."

Locke ran through procedure on his iPad, and Ikamu emailed him everything he'd figured out so far for the invitational from his phone so they could work out the details. They needed a securable area the president could watch from, where he could be protected while also feeling like one of the crowd. The agents with him were going to have to blend in. No one would relax with a bunch of suited personnel all around.

"Hey, Alana," Ikamu said. "You should surf Saturday. Show all these youngsters how it's done."

Locke said, "That's not why we'll be there."

Sure, objecting furthered her goal of getting everyone to see her as a legitimate Secret Service agent. But she was home. Despite everything that had happened so far, maybe she needed to get back to her roots.

Alana said, "After the president leaves, if it's still going on and I don't have an assignment…maybe I could."

Ikamu laughed. "I'll put you down for last." He knew she wanted to do it, but she had to make it fit her job now.

Locke sent her a look she didn't need a code breaker to decipher. She ignored his disapproval and talked through the invitational proceedings with Ikamu, asking questions Locke didn't know to ask simply because he hadn't experienced that world. Her colleague made notes and added in some questions of his own. Personnel positions, teams for each detail. Where the bathrooms and food trucks would be, so they could keep the president out of the normal flow of traffic. Where he was going to park. Ingress and egress points in case the worst happened and they had to get him out fast.

She liked when they worked like this, bouncing things off each other like they were equals.

A car pulled into the parking lot, not a beater surfer vehicle full of sand and salt water. This was a brand-new black town car. "Who—"

Ikamu's face darkened. "Yakuza."

Locke grabbed her arm. "Let's go."

EIGHT

Alana shook him off. "Hold up a second."

Locke wasn't going to stand around and wait for someone to start shooting at them. She wanted to almost die again? A drive-by was not the end he wanted for her. No way. Not when his heart felt like this. And even though it was impossible, even though it would never work with their jobs, Locke just couldn't switch off the idea of them together. More than just colleagues. More than this burgeoning friendship they seemed to be testing out lately.

"Alana." He held on to her arm, determined not to let her rush into this when there was every chance the occupants of that car would roll down the window and spray the entire beach with bullets.

The car pulled up to a stop. The window never rolled down. Instead the front passenger door opened, and a suited Asian man got out. He almost looked like a Secret Service agent but for the scar on the side of his face. He didn't spare them a single glance but moved to the rear door and opened it, watching the scenery—except for where they were. It occurred to Locke that this man didn't consider them a threat. To this man, the threat would come from elsewhere. And he had to be on guard.

Locke pulled out his phone and sent a quick text to Ray. They didn't need a crew of black-and-white police vehicles and jittery officers if they were going to get some information. But Ray would likely want to know the yakuza had approached Alana.

From the back emerged a leanly built Japanese man with an expensive haircut and a movie-star smile. This man had not grown up on the rough side of anywhere. Locke knew what that was like, and the man almost reminded him of his spoiled cousin—a little too aware of the fact that he could get whatever he wanted by expending the minimum amount of effort.

"That's Mikio Adachi." Ikamu moved behind Locke as he walked. "And my cue to leave." The Hawaiian man wandered off across the beach with a loose-legged stride.

Mikio strode over. His dress shoes clipped on the concrete of the parking lot. Locke surveyed the man as he turned his winning smile on Alana and reached his arms out. "Well, well. Alana Preston." Alana tugged on Locke until he let her go and then met the man partway.

Locke didn't let her get farther than arm's reach away from him. If Mikio tried anything he didn't like, Locke would take him down.

"Mikio." He could hear the smile in her voice. "It's really good to see you. And also kind of weird, right?"

He chuckled. "Really weird. Didn't think you'd make it back to the Big Island. But a presidential detail? That's crazy cool, Alana. Who'd have thought my old English tutor would be taking bullets for the president?"

Locke's stomach churned at the thought. "We actually try to *not* do that, if at all possible."

The man's dark eyes shifted to Locke. "Mikio Adachi." He didn't offer to shake, and all his pleasure at seeing Alana was gone in a snap.

Locke didn't offer his hand, either. "Director James Locke." Neither man disguised the fact they were sizing each other up. "Agent Preston and I have a few questions for you."

Locke's phone vibrated, one quick burst. He glanced at the screen. Ray was on his way.

Mikio looked at Alana. "Interesting company you keep. Kind of dry."

"He's not so bad."

Locke knew it was for show because, judging by her body language, this thing with Mikio was as awkward for her as it was for him. She had this stance he'd seen her use when she was unsure of herself but putting on a brave face, and she was employing it right now. Locke wanted to touch her shoulder, hold her hand or reassure her in some way, but none of that would help. Alana had to get herself through this. But there was one thing he could do.

Locke prayed for her.

"I heard what happened to you yesterday," Mikio said. "It's all over the island that Alana Preston was attacked in the water—and not by a shark."

She nodded. "After he stabbed me, he went to an elderly woman's house. Beatrice Colburn. He murdered her."

Mikio said nothing.

"We saw him in the room with her, holding the knife, Mikio." She motioned toward Locke. "The director chased the man out the window. But not before we saw the tattoo. He's yakuza."

Mikio started to shake his head. He waved her away

from the car, and Locke followed. "Things are different since my grandfather retired from the family businesses."

"You've gone legit?"

He winced. "Not exactly." Mikio's gaze drifted to Locke. "Things are better, but none of us are perfect."

"And we don't claim to be," Alana said. "But that man tried to kill me, and he did kill Beatrice."

Mikio inhaled and glanced at the steady roll of the ocean waves. For a few minutes, he was quiet, and then he said, "His name is Daniel Kaiko."

Locke entered the name on his iPad and found the file for Brian Wells. He needed to show the picture to Mikio, check for a reaction. To see what he said about this man and whether he was connected to Mikio's soldier.

"Is Daniel Kaiko one of yours?" Alana folded her arms. "Because I didn't recognize him."

"He's only been here three years. Before that he was in the navy. A SEAL, actually, but he was kicked out. He's cold. Calculating."

Locke figured it took one to recognize one—and Mikio had that streak in him. He was affable enough but could turn on a dime and become the kind of person who ran a family business that likely involved running guns, selling drugs and smuggling.

Locke said, "Do you know where he is?"

Mikio shook his head. "I haven't seen him for about a week. He said he had something to take care of, that he'd be gone for a few days."

Not good. "What about a phone number?"

"He left his phone with me. Said he needed to go off the grid."

"I'll need that phone."

Mikio's eyebrows rose. "I don't suppose you have a warrant?"

Locke doubted Mikio would readily give up a phone that could incriminate him in illegal dealings. But if anyone could convince him to hand it over, even if it was after he'd deleted everything not pertinent, it was Alana. Though, if they needed to draft an agreement that gave Mikio immunity from anything they found not related to the threat, Locke was willing to do that as well.

Alana stepped between them. "Mikio, he nearly killed me. We think he's working with another man, a marine sniper. We don't know what they're up to, but both of them have tried to kill me. If that phone can tell us anything—"

"Okay." Mikio motioned to her with his chin. "I'll give the phone to you. I might not be a good guy, but I'm not getting implicated in anything with the Secret Service. If Daniel is caught up in something, he's not taking the rest of us down with him."

So long as he could get the phone to the police and their techs could find out why Daniel Kaiko tried to kill Alana, Locke could overlook the man's tone. Still, the relationship these two clearly had—whatever they'd created years ago that was still between them—wasn't something that sat well with Locke. If Alana had been linked to the yakuza, the connection would have been thoroughly investigated when she applied for the Secret Service. Still, a person's feelings often had nothing to do with association. She could have fallen for Mikio and have no investigable ties to the man other than the fact they had gone to the same high school. Hadn't the guy mentioned that she'd been Mikio's English tutor? It could have been a smart girl's crush on a guy who was—even now—clearly a player.

Locke didn't like him at all. Even if Mikio was willing to give them the phone.

Okay, so he might be a tiny bit jealous. But he was never going to act on it, and Alana and Mikio would never know. Still, Alana had to realize there was nothing between her and this man. Aside from a shared history that meant Mikio would give her the phone.

She was a Secret Service agent now. If he had to remind her of that, he would.

Locke said, "What about Kaylee Preston? Any idea how she fits into all this?"

Alana swung around, ready to…what? What could she do in front of Mikio? A Secret Service agent didn't yell at their partner just for bringing up their baby sister in front of a dangerous man. Yeah, she wasn't under any illusions about what Mikio did for a living. The man was bad news, and the fact Ray thought he had something to do with Kaylee more than freaked her out. It terrified her.

This Mikio was not the young man she'd gone to school with. He'd grown up…grown *into* the man she saw standing in front of her. She barely even remembered him, but for that tiny slither of recognition when he'd spread his arms wide. They'd always hugged. He'd been affectionate, but it was only part of the persona he'd played at school—the persona of an extrovert football captain.

Alana cleared her throat. "Ray said—"

Mikio waved off what she'd been about to say. He'd

done that when he knew the answer, and it had freaked a lot of people out that he was so street-smart. "I don't know what she has to do with Daniel. Kaylee fits into this because we're seeing each other. Daniel doesn't like her, but he would never accept a reporter. He thinks she's a liability, and he told me so. Repeatedly. At least until I convinced him I'd heard what he was saying."

That confirmed it, then. Ray knew. Mikio told them. Her sister was dating him, and she'd never be able to warn Kaylee that Mikio wasn't a good guy. At least not in a way that Kaylee would believe it was coming from a legitimate place of caring for her. Not when Kaylee hated her for whatever reason Alana didn't understand and had screamed at her until Alana did what her sister asked and "got out of her life."

"If he didn't like her," Locke said, "is it possible Daniel would try and hurt Kaylee?"

Alana glanced at him. Did he think Kaylee was hurt? The shock of that idea hit her like a static discharge—sharp and fast—and was over just as quickly. There was no way she was hurt, otherwise Ray or Mikio would have known.

"She isn't hurt." But that didn't mean Alana knew where her sister was. "Is she?"

"I don't know." Mikio's face flashed with concern. "She was supposed to meet me for dinner last night, but she never showed up."

"Have you called her?"

He frowned at Locke's question. "I do not pursue women, and I do not get stood up. That woman is an anomaly. However, if she can't be present, then I'm done with her."

Alana nearly slapped him. Seriously?

Locke put a hand on her arm. But maybe he should let her hit Mikio in his smug face. It would probably make her feel better.

Alana said, "You aren't worried something happened to her?"

Mikio shrugged one shoulder. "Kaylee told me she'd stumbled onto a big story. Work is very important to her, probably more important than me, although that's not what she claims. When Kaylee gets wind of a big story, she sometimes disappears for a couple of days. It's not unusual, and I've learned to get on with things. She just usually doesn't make plans she might have to break."

Alana honestly felt sad for the man. Mikio couldn't go soft over a woman or it would likely ruin his standing within the Japanese mafia. But if Kaylee had done this to him before, that meant she'd come back and patched things up with him. Their relationship had been through this cycle already, and he hadn't moved on yet. Not if they were still together.

She just hoped Kaylee knew what she was doing getting in a relationship with a man like this. The yakuza would never let him go, and maybe he didn't want to be free of them. It would be a hard road, going the distance in a relationship where neither party could be fully committed. They both had ties elsewhere.

Alana wished she could talk to her sister about it to see how she was doing, if she was happy. Perhaps she hadn't shown up to dinner because she wanted to end things with Mikio. Her absence didn't mean Daniel had killed her, or that she was somewhere hurt. Right?

Locke tugged on Alana's elbow until she stepped closer to him. "I think this navy SEAL guy, Daniel, might have thought you were Kaylee and tried to hurt you."

"You think he mistook me for her?" She glanced at Mikio, who seemed interested.

Locke swiped the screen of his iPad and showed her a picture of her sister's Facebook page. Kaylee had the same hairstyle. "I think it's possible he knew it was you and intended to kill you—or scare you—but we can't rule out mistaken identity, either, Alana. Not until we know for sure."

Alana nodded. "Okay, I guess not."

"He seemed surprised at Beatrice Colburn's house, surprised that it was you. Or surprised that you were there." Locke swiped on the screen again, then turned it so Mikio could see. "This is Brian Wells. He's a military sniper. A marine. We think he also tried to kill Alana in that restaurant shooting last night."

Mikio studied the screen, but she didn't see any recognition there. Alana said, "If they're both navy maybe they knew each other in the service? There's a slim chance, but it's possible their paths crossed."

Locke glanced at her. "That's a good lead. One of the best ones we've had so far." He turned back to Mikio to ask another question, but a police car pulled up behind the yakuza vehicle. Ray, in his uniform, climbed out, hand resting on his gun. Mikio's men braced, but Mikio lifted a hand to hold them off. Ray taunted them with a wave, and Mikio's men all bristled.

Ray said, "Where's Kaylee, Mikio?"

The yakuza boss lifted both hands. "I don't know where your sister is, as I've already told your lovely *other* sister." He motioned to Alana.

Ray didn't look at her. Alana would never understand

those man stances, the interplay that didn't seem to require words. Something Locke referred to as a "threat assessment," like it was a quantifiable thing to just get a bad feeling about someone. Maybe it really was a man thing.

She lifted both hands, palms out. "Guys." She wasn't going to get in the middle of their power play. "Can't we ping Kaylee's phone or something?"

Ray said, "It's not giving out a signal—it's either turned off or the battery is dead."

It was the way he said *dead* that got her. Alana took a step back. Locke was immediately beside her, right by her shoulder. He didn't touch her, but his presence had the same effect. He was her support when she needed it. It was nice, but she couldn't rely on him. Locke wasn't always going to be there to support her—not with family drama that hadn't changed in years.

Locke said, "Agent Preston and I should be going." He paused, all his attention on Mikio. Likely doing his own *threat assessment*. "Get us that phone."

Mikio nodded. He turned to leave, but Ray got in his way. "I'm not done talking to you."

Alana heard the yakuza boss sigh as she followed Locke toward the vehicle. They drove back to the neighborhood where Kaylee lived.

"I don't know where else to look. It's probably pointless to keep coming back to her house, but it's all I've got." She didn't want to admit she didn't know that much about her sister these days.

Locke shut the engine off. "It's a good idea, Alana."

Back to her first name. She was getting whiplash with all the back-and-forth, but at the same time realized he saved her first name for when it was just the two of them. Something personal.

The thought stuck with her as they ascended the stairs to Kaylee's apartment. His hand reached out to ring the doorbell.

Someone screamed.

Alana drew her weapon, and Locke did the same. He motioned that he would go first and stepped in front of her.

NINE

Locke kicked the door open. Gun raised, his finger resting straight along the barrel as he moved down the hall. Alana was behind him. He could hear the push of each breath and prayed they wouldn't find a similar scene to what they'd stumbled on in Beatrice's house.

Locke moved his finger to the trigger as he emerged into the living room–kitchen–dining room of the small one-bedroom apartment. Old couches with a million pillows and blankets, a clean kitchen that needed serious updates, and a huge messy desk where he'd have put the dining table. In the center a woman with long dark hair and Alana's build was tied to her office chair. A man stood behind her.

"Kaylee." Alana breathed her sister's name.

Locke shifted his stance so he and Alana were side by side. There was no way she was going to face the man who held a knife on Kaylee Preston by herself.

"Put the weapon down, Daniel." The man's eyes widened at Locke's use of his name. It was him, no doubt. The man he'd chased from Beatrice Colburn's house was Daniel Kaiko. "And back away from the woman."

Kaylee had been cut, short nicks in her shirt that had

dampened the material. Not deep enough that they bled profusely, but enough that they'd sting. Considering the man was a SEAL, Locke figured it was a technique he'd picked up before he was fired from the service. Now he was using it on Alana's sister.

But for what? If he was questioning her instead of just killing her quickly, that meant he thought Kaylee had information.

Daniel hadn't moved, and he hadn't dropped the knife. He stood close to Kaylee, the blade still at the ready.

"Daniel—"

Before Locke could finish, the ex-SEAL grabbed Kaylee's hair with his free hand. Her face lifted and he pressed the knife tip beneath her chin.

Alana let out a little whine of frustration. Locke was powerless as well, unable to do much to help this woman who could die if they made the wrong move. Locke could imagine what it would be like if it was one of his sisters here, held at knifepoint. But that probably didn't touch what Alana was feeling right now, actually seeing her younger sister like this.

"Both of you back off." He shifted his grip on her hair and Kaylee sucked in a breath. "Or I slit her throat."

Locke reached his arm out in front of Alana. He took a step back and moved her with him. "We're back. Let her go and we'll talk about this." What they were going to figure out, he didn't know. Daniel Kaiko was going to jail, and that was about the end of it. No discussion required.

Daniel's eyes narrowed. "Put your guns down, kick them to me and I leave. No harm, no foul."

Sure, it seemed like Kaylee would feel that way about

it. Locke didn't like sarcasm, but the woman was pale and sweating, her breath coming fast. Her eyes darted between Locke and Alana, imploring them to do something. To help her.

Alana's gun started to lower. Locke shook his head but didn't turn or look at her. He couldn't take his eyes off this guy. "We aren't disarming ourselves, Daniel. You are. Now put the knife down and let Kaylee go."

Daniel shifted almost imperceptibly. Locke had dealt with nervous, twitchy assailants who didn't care who got hurt. Cool and calculated was rare but not unprecedented, given this man had been trained as a SEAL.

With the knife still at Kaylee's throat, Daniel twisted his other shoulder back. His hand went behind him, then came back up holding a pistol.

Daniel fired, but Kaylee rolled her chair into him and his shot went wide. Locke and Alana returned fire. Alana missed.

Daniel stumbled, and the red stain of the wound from Locke's bullet spread across his shoulder. He dropped the knife and pressed his hand against his chest, high on his shirt. The gun fell to the floor. Daniel stumbled back one step but didn't go down. He perched on the edge of the desk.

Locke moved to him and kicked the gun aside. Then kicked away the knife. He held aim on the man and pulled his phone out, called 9-1-1 for officers and an ambulance, then made a second call. Ray's name made Alana turn and give him a look in the middle of untying her sister. He explained the situation, and the sergeant promised to be there in minutes.

Thank You, Lord. They'd only just learned Daniel Kaiko's identity. There had been no time to look him up or find any leads as to his whereabouts. And here he was. Surely Ray and Mikio had come here to find Kaylee, but maybe they'd only left her voice mails. Who simply knocked on someone's door these days? At least without calling or messaging the person, as well.

Locke didn't turn, but spoke over his shoulder. "She okay?" When his partner didn't answer, he said, "Alana?"

It wasn't her voice he heard, but her sister's. "I didn't need your help. I was handling it."

Locke wasn't going to get in the middle of their family drama. All he said was, "An ambulance is coming. When the cops get this guy out of here, we'll get you medical attention."

"Hey, I need stitches," Daniel Kaiko whined.

Locke eyed the former SEAL. "I hear they have good medical care in prison."

Daniel sneered. "Won't matter if I'm in prison or not."

"We'll find Brian Wells. Don't you worry."

His eyes widened in a tiny flash of movement, and then his face blanked. They knew his partner's name, and it surprised him. But Locke wanted to watch him squirm. "Why did you try to kill Alana? What do you want from Kaylee, and what does all this have to do with Brian?"

Daniel's attention flicked to Kaylee.

"Eyes on me," Locke demanded. "And answer the question."

He sneered. "Which one?"

Locke didn't have time to answer. The police entered, ones he hadn't met before. They surveyed the scene, and then one went back to the front door. "It's clear."

Two EMTs wheeled a stretcher in. By the time they found Brian Wells, would Locke and Alana have seen every cop and paramedic on this island?

He let the thought go and backed up, introduced himself and Alana, and let the officers take over with Daniel. Locke explained everything about the man, and how he'd tried to stab Alana the morning before. The raised eyebrows weren't a surprise. He should've known everywhere on this island people would react like that to hearing her name. He waited while they cuffed the former SEAL and one checked the wound on his shoulder. The officer glanced at Locke. "This your doing?"

He nodded. "Daniel fired first." Locke surveyed the wall behind where he and Alana had entered. The hallway, the ceiling. He strode to the hole beside a framed photo. "Right there." The bullet was lodged in the wall.

"I'll get the crime-scene guys in here." They moved with Daniel toward the door. "You wanna talk to this guy after we get him seen at the hospital and then booked?"

"Yes." Daniel was their best shot at finding Brian Wells. Hopefully he'd be more forthcoming in the interrogation room, where Locke would have more time to wait for answers.

The officers left with Daniel, and Alana walked over to him. He looked beyond her to where her sister lay. The EMTs were working, but Kaylee Preston's face was turned away.

Locke glanced at his partner. "You okay?"

"Why does it seem like you've asked me that a hundred times today?" He didn't smile. Alana sighed. He knew she was just avoiding talking about the obvious.

But she'd tried to engage her sister, tried to help her, and Kaylee had brushed her off. Brushed Alana's hand from her shoulder even though the action made her wince. Dismissed Alana's concern—and her questions.

How were they supposed to find out how Kaylee was involved when Alana's sister wouldn't even talk to her? Not just obstinate, Kaylee was acting hurt, like it was Alana who had left. Which she had, but only because Kaylee told her to *go*. As though in doing what Kaylee had asked, somehow Alana had betrayed her.

It made no sense.

Alana didn't want to talk about it with Locke. Something had happened today, and she wasn't sure she'd describe it as their having grown closer, but it was definitely not like it had been between them before. It was almost as if they were on their way to becoming friends.

If she'd been told months ago that this would happen, she'd have laughed.

The EMTs got Kaylee onto a stretcher. She immediately turned so Alana couldn't see her face. Kaylee didn't want to talk. Didn't want help. They wheeled her out.

"You aren't going to go with her?"

When she looked at Locke, she didn't see disappointment—which was something, at least—she only saw curiosity. Yes, they were working, but this constituted a family emergency. Still, Alana said, "She doesn't want me."

"She told you that?"

Alana nodded and glanced around. "Let's take a look." She wandered to the desk. "Maybe all this has to do with what Kaylee was working on. Mikio said it was a big story." She didn't think this was just because Daniel didn't like Mikio's choice of girlfriend.

"Right, she's a reporter."

"For the Hilo *Explorer*." The slight smile curled her lips. Despite their estrangement, she was proud of what her sister had achieved and had read the online edition since Kaylee was hired there.

Alana looked through the mess of papers on her sister's desk and jiggled the mouse. Under a stack of bills was a book about the Kennedy assassination. Then one about Lincoln. Alana frowned and kept leafing through papers. Maybe Kaylee read books about presidents for the same reason Alana read the newspaper Kaylee worked for.

The computer monitor flicked on, the desktop background a picture of Ray, Alana and Kaylee from years ago, camping on Maui. Their dad had taken it.

The sight of it hit her in a way she hadn't been expecting. Her sister *had* to care about her if Kaylee had her family on her computer where she'd see the picture every day. Kaylee claimed she didn't want anything to do with Alana now, but then there was this. Maybe it was all just bravado that covered up what she was really feeling—hurt and missing her family. Alana needed to talk to Ray about it, or maybe even Mikio.

There had to be a way to get through to Kaylee, and not just because they needed information from her. Kaylee didn't want to be interrogated, even if it was only questions that were fired at her. She'd been through a traumatic experience, but so had Alana. There had to be some common ground to be found there, as they'd both been attacked with a knife.

Locke reached past her, unaware of the fact she was

having a mental breakdown. That or he just figured she didn't want him to know about it. Alana sucked in a breath and walked over to perch on the back of the couch the way their father had never allowed them to do. These were his couches. She recognized them now underneath all the pillows and blankets Kaylee had decorated with.

What else did her sister have of their past that she'd held onto?

"Her web history is a lot of sites with information about presidential security measures. Vacations the president has been on, incidents that've happened in the past. Gunmen running onto the south lawn of the White House, that kind of thing." He frowned, clicking through windows on her sister's browser. "She even looked you up, though I don't know if she tied the four who answered the ad to the president's visit. Or how she might have."

Alana said, "Anything about assassinations?"

Locke clicked through screens. "Not that I can see. A couple of military websites. An online buy/sell forum— maybe she was looking for a new lamp. A social media community page for a division of the marines that were stationed in Japan… Huh."

"What?" She pushed off the couch, completely drained. She'd been running on adrenaline most of the past two days, but the rush had gone and now she was hitting a wall despite the full night of sleep she'd had last night.

"Could be a link between Brian Wells and Daniel Kaiko, their service in Japan, but we'll have to confirm that with the navy." He straightened and looked at her. "I'll call in to Secret Service intelligence and have them check to see if Wells and Kaiko were ever stationed at the same naval base."

He continued, "Looks like she also visited Daniel's personal page." He paused. "And there's something else."

"What?" Alana moved closer. He clicked again, and the website for the surf competition came up. "Maybe she was planning to attend."

"Or all this is connected," he said. "Whichever it is, we really need to talk to her."

"I know." Alana sighed. "Maybe you could go in there. It's possible she'll talk to you."

"What about Ray?"

She opened her mouth to answer, but her brother strode through the apartment door at that moment. "What about me?"

Locke held out his hand and they shook. "I was just saying that maybe you could talk to Kaylee. She might be willing to tell you what all this means." He motioned to the computer.

"I can try," Ray said. "If it's going to shed some light on Beatrice Colburn's murder, I can get the paperwork put through and have her computer taken in. Our techs can look at it."

Alana winced. She doubted Kaylee would want someone she didn't know leafing through every file on her hard drive. That was way too intrusive. "Maybe Daniel Kaiko will tell us what we need to know."

"I'd rather not let Kaylee off that easily if we can help it." Ray folded his arms.

"What do you mean?" Alana motioned to the chair. "Kaylee was tied up and tortured. Held at knifepoint. That isn't my definition of getting off easily."

"That's not what I mean, Lana."

The nickname he hadn't used for years washed over her. But it only made her feel a *little* better.

Ray continued, oblivious to what was going on with her. "I just mean that if we have the opportunity to get through to her, I say we use it. Otherwise she's going to keep shutting us both out."

Alana didn't know what to say. She glanced at Locke and saw his gaze on her. He looked entirely too perceptive for her taste. If she wasn't careful, he was going to start putting in his two cents on her family dynamic. She didn't need his help. Alana was doing fine on her own—just like everyone wanted.

She decided to make the decision herself. "Let's go to the hospital. One of us should try to talk to her. I don't want to go through her things any more than we already have. Not if we don't have to."

Locke nodded.

Ray said, "I'll stay and wait for the crime-scene guys."

Alana said, "Okay," to her brother, and then led the way. She didn't want to stay in there much longer. All she could think about was finding her sister. That knife.

She glanced back at Locke on the stairs. He opened his mouth to speak, but she said, "Don't ask me if I'm okay."

Locke raised both hands. He drove them to the hospital, and neither spoke much. When they exited the elevator on the floor where her sister had been assigned, he touched her elbow. "I'm going to send an email and listen to my messages."

Alana nodded.

She found her sister's room easily, as it was the one

with police officers stationed outside. Apparently Ray thought it necessary to keep her under guard. After she gave them her name, the officer frowned. He reached into the breast pocket on his uniform shirt and pulled out a folded paper. "Your sister talked to the Lieutenant, but she's refusing any other visitors."

Alana figured as much.

He handed her the paper. "She said if you or Sergeant Preston came by that I should hand you this."

She said thanks and wandered back toward Locke while the officer muttered something about being a messenger boy. Alana unfolded the paper and found a list of four names scrawled in pencil in her sister's handwriting.

"Locke. Come take a look at this."

TEN

Locke ended his call and came to stand beside her. "What is it, Alana?"

She showed him the paper in her hand. "The cop gave me a note—it's from Kaylee." There was more, as far as he could see, but she didn't share.

Locke figured she understood there were more important things at play than her strained relationship with her sister, whom she hadn't gone in to see. He'd watched Alana's exchange with the officer. The man's disgruntled handing over of the paper. Her clear disappointment. It made him want to comfort her, but there was no time for that, either.

"What's on the note?" When she gave it to him, he read off the list of four names that had been penciled in a shaky but distinctly feminine hand. "Beatrice Colburn. Daniel Kaiko. Brian Wells. Zane Franks."

Alana said, "We know who the other three are, but who is Zane Franks?"

"It sounds familiar." He scrolled through his contacts and found the number for Secret Service intelligence. "I'm going to make a call. Depending on what I find out, we should be ready to move. Are you done here?"

"No." She frowned at him, like she couldn't believe he'd suggest such a thing.

"I know you don't *want* to be done, Alana, but is there anything you can really do here right now?"

Alana sighed. "Let's go. You can make your call, and I'll just do what you say. Never mind that my personal life is a complete disaster."

"Alana." He stepped closer, his voice low. "We can talk about it. But this isn't the right time." She should pray, too, but he didn't figure she'd take that idea too well right now. He had to tread carefully, or he'd turn her off to the idea of faith and she'd never even look into it for herself.

She brushed past him. "Who says I want to talk about it?"

What she didn't say was *with you*, but he heard the words anyway. Locke rode the elevator with her and then called intelligence when they reached the lobby. When the agent answered the phone, Locke asked about Zane Franks.

He heard the fast click of typing in the background. "Franks. Franks. Yep, he's one of ours."

"What do you mean?" He saw Alana glance over at his question, but kept his attention on the phone and the act of scanning the area around them for Brian Wells. The last thing he wanted was to get shot with a sniper round right outside the hospital. That wasn't in his five-year plan, and he doubted it was part of Alana's, either.

"Zane Franks was on our list."

"In Hawaii?"

"No, he's from Denver."

"That's where I remember the name." Locke had been sick the last time the president went to Denver, so he'd missed that detail. Agents would have made the standard advance team visit, as he and Alana tried to do with Beatrice yesterday, but Locke didn't go on that trip.

"Franks was cleared the last time we saw him, and his job was moving him to Hawaii." The agent read off the address to Locke. "But the man is seventy-six, so there isn't a lot he could do outside of the power he wields in the boardroom." The agent paused. "You aren't calling because of your visit to him, are you?"

"The president is already here. Franks wasn't on our list, and the final visits were done yesterday before Air Force One landed. Still, I can't help feeling like something serious is going on." He explained what had happened the last couple of days.

"Why were we not notified of any of this?"

"What do you mean? I passed it all to Director William Matthews and followed up with my email reports. Intelligence was copied in."

"I have nothing about Beatrice Colburn being *dead*. The report I have says that you signed off on her after the visit."

Locke gaped. "She was dead, and we chased her murderer from the house."

"That is *not* what I have."

How was it possible that the reports he'd sent in had been…what, changed? Doctored, somehow? This was unreal. "Why on earth would someone go to the trouble of altering my report to make it sound like everything is fine?"

Alana waited by the car, but Locke didn't click the button or move to get in. He could barely think. How was he supposed to unravel this? He had to, though, because there was absolutely, for sure, something strange going on.

And it put the president's life in danger.

The agent said, "The only reason I can think of is that everything is not fine."

Locke nodded. Alana waited patiently for him to explain. He told the agent, "I have to talk to Director Matthews, but you'll need to follow up on your end. Otherwise my concerns will only get buried again."

Because that's what was happening. Multiple times he'd had concerns, a bad feeling in his gut about this visit. William had brushed it off, but Locke couldn't help thinking there was more going on. Now they had a solid link between all involved. There had to be more than they were seeing.

He continued, "I'll get copies of my emails resent so that you can see the originals. Have them looked at—I want forensics going through my phone, iPad and my computer, and all of your systems." He took a breath. "And I'll talk to the president about this. If there's something brewing here, then he can't stay. We'll have to move up the timetable and get him out of Hawaii before the worst happens."

"Copy that." The intelligence agent hung up.

Locke explained everything to Alana even as he found the number in his contacts for an agent on William's team who would—hopefully—be with the president right now. *God, we need Your help. The president could be in danger, and someone is colluding against us. Help us figure this out.* He hit the button to dial and…saw the screen. *No signal.* "How can I have no signal right now? I was just on the phone."

Alana got her phone from her belt. "Me, too. No signal. That's weird."

"Maybe it isn't just us. Maybe it's a weird dead spot." Did he really believe that? He clicked the locks and got in the car. "Let's get to the conference center. We can warn them in person that something is going on."

Alana nodded and buckled her seat belt. He had her go back through emails on his iPad and look for the reports he'd copied William on, the ones he'd sent to intelligence. She opened each one and read aloud what he'd completed.

Locke shook his head. "That isn't what I wrote. Try to find the original file." An idea hit him. "Wait. Does the iPad have signal?"

"Yes. It does."

"Message Agent Carlsen. Tell him we believe the president might be in danger."

She typed. Faster than he could in his two-thumbed method. Alana pressed Send, and he pulled out of the hospital parking lot onto the street.

Eyes still on the screen, Alana said, "Message failed." She looked up then. "It didn't go through." She tried to make a call on her cell phone and then his again. Neither worked. "This is super weird. Something…or someone…is blocking us from contacting anyone."

"This isn't good."

She nodded her agreement. They were coming up on a chain pharmacy, so Locke pulled in and parked. They strode inside together, and he flashed his badge at the bored clerk behind the cash register. "I need to use your phone."

She handed him the cell from her pocket. He'd been talking about the landline in the store but didn't quibble.

Locke called 9-1-1, identified himself and told the operator he had good reason to believe that the president's life was in imminent danger.

* * *

Alana wanted to rush over to the conference center. What was so bad about that?

Locke hadn't stopped shaking his head since she suggested it. "It's a good idea, but there will be so much security, so much chaos if they're evacuating POTUS, that if we show up, we'll just get in the way. And it's not our detail. The president has enough Secret Service agents surrounding him already, and we have to trust them the same way that they trust us. So we're better off investigating this."

"Okay." She folded her arms, still not convinced others should protect the president in person when it was their job, as well. Wasn't this an all-hands-on-deck situation? "So what do we do instead?"

"We go to Zane Franks's house. We also need to call Ray and find out if Daniel Kaiko has talked yet."

"Which one first?" He was letting her drive this time, since they traded off that job.

"Zane." He gave her the address. "We can make the call after. A man's life is in danger."

Alana knew where it was, so she waved off his offer of a map.

"Good, because it isn't loading."

"Is someone messing with our tech?"

Locke's face was dark. "They messed with my emails. Somehow got to the original files and made it so that I sent their version instead of mine." He shook his head. "It's a wonder William didn't get back with me if the report I apparently sent him indicated that everything was fine and I explained at Beatrice's house that things were not."

"He did brush it off on the phone when you tried to tell him there was a problem."

Locke nodded. "This whole thing has been weird, but I guess he didn't bother reading the follow-up report after we spoke. Who actually reads every email they're copied on? Maybe William doesn't know what the report said."

Alana said, "But that doesn't explain why intelligence thought Beatrice was alive. Or who messed with the report in your email."

He paused. "I don't want to think William might have something to do with all this, but I can't let it go. If Zane doesn't have a phone, then we'll find somewhere else to call from again. We need to know they got the president out of the conference center. But if Franks is part of this, we have to find him and detain him."

They also had to find Brian Wells. Beatrice was dead, and Daniel was in police custody. "There has to be some kind of link between the four of them for Kaylee to have put them all on that paper." Alana continued to air her thoughts aloud. "Maybe we can figure out what the connection is beyond that phone number on the ad in Brian's house that's also on Beatrice's call history.

"Wells and Kaiko were both in the navy, but Beatrice wasn't. She had bomb schematics, and Daniel killed her. Maybe she's on the list because she had a part to play in it, but she isn't fully connected the way the first two men we've come across seem to be. They could have simply intended on using her bomb so that the signature sent the investigators directly back to her."

"Good questions."

Locke had as many answers as she did, which wasn't many. For the first time, she was anxious to follow his lead instead of determined to be in his shoes. She would be, one day, if she stuck with it. She would have the Secret Service career she wanted. But for now things were so confusing that she was happy to be the one with the director for a mentor, instead of the one who took all the responsibility.

He said, "If you were shopping for a team to organize a plot, who better than the ones on our list? People with experience."

"But they're the first ones we would look at if something did happen while the president was here."

Locke worked his mouth from side to side. "True. It doesn't make much sense."

Alana pulled up outside Zane Franks's residence—a single-wide trailer probably billed as a "beach house." The investment company he worked for had sent him here to seal a deal for them, and in the meantime Franks was living the dream on the edge of the ocean. The trailer was older, though neat, but his sunrise view must've been incredible.

She turned to Locke. "I just want to say…" Suddenly it seemed dumb to tell him, but she forged on regardless. "Thank you, I guess. Thank you for being here, because I don't know how I'd handle this if you weren't. Everything that's happened the past couple of days. You've been with me through it all, and I just wanted you to know that I appreciate it, Locke."

His face softened. Had she ever seen that look before? "You're welcome, Alana."

Her stomach, the spot where she'd been cut by Daniel Kaiko's knife, didn't feel great. Okay, it hurt kind of a lot. She was exhausted, and Locke didn't look much better. Though she had a feeling the grim expression he'd defaulted back to was probably about the possible threat to the president and not what was happening to

YOUR PARTICIPATION IS REQUESTED!

Dear Reader,

Since you are a lover of our books – we would like to get to know you!

Inside you will find a short Reader's Survey. Sharing your answers with us will help our editorial staff understand who you are and what activities you enjoy.

To thank you for your participation, we would like to send you 2 books and 2 gifts – **ABSOLUTELY FREE!**

Enjoy your gifts with our appreciation,

Pam Powers

SEE INSIDE FOR READER'S SURVEY

For Your Reading Pleasure...

We'll send you 2 books and 2 gifts
ABSOLUTELY FREE
just for completing our Reader's Survey!

YOURS FREE!
We'll send you two fabulous surprise gifts absolutely FREE, just for trying our books!

Visit us at:
www.ReaderService.com

YOUR READER'S SURVEY
"THANK YOU" FREE GIFTS INCLUDE:
- ▶ **2 FREE** books
- ▶ **2 lovely surprise gifts**

PLEASE FILL IN THE CIRCLES COMPLETELY TO RESPOND

1) What type of fiction books do you enjoy reading? (Check all that apply)
○ Suspense/Thrillers ○ Action/Adventure ○ Modern-day Romances
○ Historical Romance ○ Humor ○ Paranormal Romance

2) What attracted you most to the last fiction book you purchased on impulse?
○ The Title ○ The Cover ○ The Author ○ The Story

3) What is usually the greatest influencer when you <u>plan</u> to buy a book?
○ Advertising ○ Referral ○ Book Review

4) How often do you access the internet?
○ Daily ○ Weekly ○ Monthly ○ Rarely or never

5) How many NEW paperback fiction novels have you purchased in the past 3 months?
○ 0 - 2 ○ 3 - 6 ○ 7 or more

YES! I have completed the Reader's Survey. Please send me 2 FREE books and 2 FREE gifts (gifts are worth about $10 retail). I understand that I am under no obligation to purchase any books, as explained on the back of this card.

❏ I prefer the regular-print edition   ❏ I prefer the larger-print edition
153/353 IDL GMRH   107/307 IDL GMRH

FIRST NAME	LAST NAME

ADDRESS

APT.#	CITY

STATE/PROV.	ZIP/POSTAL CODE

SLI-817-SCT17

READER SERVICE—Here's how it works:

BUSINESS REPLY MAIL

FIRST-CLASS MAIL   PERMIT NO. 717   BUFFALO, NY

POSTAGE WILL BE PAID BY ADDRESSEE

READER SERVICE
PO BOX 1341
BUFFALO NY 14240-8571

NO POSTAGE
NECESSARY
IF MAILED
IN THE
UNITED STATES

them. He was just that kind of Secret Service agent—the selfless kind she wanted to be one day.

For now she had far too much distracting her attention from focusing on her job. Part of that was the safe feeling she'd known around Locke since he tackled her in the restaurant. As much as she'd complained—though she still felt that she should have reacted faster—really she was grateful for him being there.

"If any of this is my fault—" She paused, not sure how to explain it other than to say, "Well, things have been happening, and they seem to involve me. My family. I just want to say I'm sorry if I've dragged you into something that's my doing."

Locke shook his head. "I genuinely think Daniel mistook you for your sister, realized it and then went after her. He's working with Brian Wells, and the two of them still wanted you off their scent. Hence the restaurant shooting. Beatrice had bomb schematics they wanted, so they pulled her in. Maybe she turned them down so they killed her for it, or maybe that was the plan all along. Maybe it's just a two-man show." He grabbed his door handle. "But maybe not. So let's go see how Zane Franks fits into it all, yeah?"

"Yeah."

She met up with Locke on the sidewalk and kept pace with him. He was her example of how to be a good Secret Service agent—professional, cool under stress and able to handle even the craziest situations. He hadn't freaked out at all since this happened. He'd been in a fight and had been shot at when she was. So why did it feel like he wanted to take care of her?

She needed to be more like him. Roll with the situation. Process it and set it aside. Her sister didn't want to talk to her, and she had to deal with that later. Right now it was work time.

The door was ajar.

Alana whispered, "Maybe our sniper is in there."

But he wasn't. When they stepped inside, they found Zane Franks on the floor of his living room, dead from a gunshot wound to his forehead and another in his chest.

"Execution style," Locke muttered.

Alana hadn't needed to know that. The smell… She sucked in a breath and tried to find some clean air, but it was everywhere. To distract herself she looked around, looked at the return addresses on his mail, junk and magazines. Found a newspaper.

"Locke?"

She glanced over, and he waved her off, a corded phone to his ear. "Yes, ma'am. He's dead. And I need Sergeant Ray Preston. Yes, thank you." Seconds later Locke said, "Ray. Thank You, God—" He was cut off, probably by whatever her brother was saying. "You're kidding me. They really think that?"

Locke squeezed the bridge of his nose. "Well, I'm at the scene of another murder, so there's my alibi for you." He paused. "No. He was dead when we got here." Locke sighed. "Okay, thanks."

He hung up. "Ray will be here in a minute, but when he is, it won't be to deal with Mr. Franks. It'll be to arrest me."

Alana said, "What?"

Locke nodded, the confusion on his face reflecting hers. "It's all over the police band that I called in a bomb threat. Only they're broadcasting it like I'm the one who set the bomb." He swallowed. "They think I want to kill the president."

ELEVEN

Dread washed over him, but Locke kept his gaze on Alana. He wanted her reaction. He needed it. But it wasn't surprise he got. Alana spun around, spun back and then said, "We should get out of here."

"Don't want to face your brother?"

"He's going to arrest you!" Her eyes were wild. She reminded him of one of his sisters when they found out Mom had fallen while they were at the store. Wendy had taken him to spend some of his birthday money... until her phone rang. The fear and worry had manifested itself in a kind of manic state. He'd had to help her control it—even though he'd only been ten—until they reached the hospital to meet everyone. For whatever reason, God had created him as the kind of person who expressed less the greater the emotion, not more.

"Why are you just standing there? Let's go!"

"I don't like leaving a body." It didn't sit well with him.

"We can shut the front door."

"No, we found it open. We'll be able to tell Ray we left the place exactly as we found it." He eased it back with his foot until it was slightly ajar and then they headed for the car. "Maybe it's a blessing our phones aren't working. That way no one can track us."

Alana got hers out. "Yep. Still no signal. Is someone blocking them?"

"Could be. If it's just us, they'd have to either be local and jamming them, or they could have had someone from the phone company with access to our lines hack us." He shook his head. "We're supposed to have devices that are extra secure."

"Is it Brian Wells?"

"He's a sniper, which makes me sure the restaurant shooting was him. Hacking phones is a whole different thing, not to mention changing the report that I emailed. I'd believe Daniel Kaiko could do this, but we'd have to access his service record to see what his particular skills are. Plus he'd have to know what extra safeguards the Secret Service uses. But he's in police custody."

"So there's someone else involved, then? But they've killed the other two people on the list. Which leaves my sister, who wrote it."

Locke grabbed her hand and squeezed it. He ignored the surprised look on her face and unlocked the car. He held the door for her, just because he wanted to. It was a routine part of their job, but not an action they performed for each other. Still, he took pleasure in the simplicity of doing it now, for Alana.

Locke drove a mile without thinking too much about where they were headed. They only needed to get out of the area where Zane Franks's house was. He parked and tried his phone again, calling an agent on his team first. The man was with the president now, having been assigned as extra personnel for tonight's event at the conference center. But there was no answer.

Locke tried William next, and while he waited for it to connect, he said to Alana, "Once I talk to someone, I'm sure the whole thing will be cleared up. They know me. Why would they think I'd call in to say I'm bombing the conference center instead of the fact I'm aware of an active threat? They can't think it's for real."

"That makes sense."

Not much about this did. He opened his mouth to say as much, when his phone did nothing. Locke threw it in the cup holder. "I can't get through to anyone."

"Maybe we should go to the convention center."

He thought through what he knew of the event and the schedule of the president's entrance and exit. There wasn't a good time for them to interrupt and take William's attention from protecting the president. Besides, when they'd gotten the call Locke made from the pharmacy, they would likely have rushed the president out of the building to a prearranged secure location. After that they'd head back to the hotel while police scoured the conference center to try to locate the bomb.

He said, "It's better if we wait until they run out the procedure for a threat like that. After they've looked for the bomb, we can explain that it was some kind of misunderstanding of what I said over the phone. The pharmacy clerk can back me up, and the dispatcher I told about Zane being dead. Otherwise we put the president's safety in jeopardy."

"So where do we go?"

Locke shifted in his seat. "You don't have to come with me."

"What do you mean?"

"Just that…if Ray is out to arrest me, maybe you should go back and talk to him. You can tell my side of the story. They'll know that you had nothing to do with it even though you were with me."

"It might be worth it to convince them they got it wrong, but I don't like the idea of splitting up." She shook her head. "Not at all."

"So we're in this together?"

"Yes."

Locke said, "Not if it's going to kill your career."

"And it's okay if it kills yours?"

"Isn't just one better than both of us?"

She couldn't argue with that. Alana might not like the situation, and she might want to stick together out of some sense of camaraderie. Or that fierce determination she had to be seen as a capable agent. Whichever reason it was, Locke didn't want her to stay with him for any of *those* reasons. He wanted her there only if it was where she wanted to be.

"You want to be alone in this?" Alana lifted her hands. "It could get cleared up in thirty minutes, or it could be career ending. You don't know. And until we have the answer, I'm staying right here."

She almost looked like she was about to cry. Locke didn't like that at all, so he fell back on his old tactic of teasing. It had worked in the past, sometimes.

"You're staying on this street?"

She didn't answer.

"In the car?"

Alana folded her arms. "You know what I mean."

"I do. And I'm trusting God will work this out quickly, that He'll take care of me. If that means more bad has to happen, that's going to be part of how He works things out. So if it gets worse, don't worry, Alana. It doesn't mean He's left us, it only means it's not time for us to be through this yet." He paused. "And for the record, thank you for sticking with me."

"It's helped so far." She frowned. "Have you been praying this whole time?"

He nodded. "I have."

"We went to this tiny church on the beach when we were kids. I guess I haven't thought about it for a long time. But if it's working, it can't hurt."

Locke still didn't know why she wanted to be here with him, but he was grateful for it anyway. "We could head to the hospital, see if we can talk to your sister without getting arrested by the officers guarding her. Maybe she'll answer my questions in an official interview. She won't be able to say no because of her issues with you."

They could try to talk with Daniel, but they'd have to get past the police officers stationed outside his room. It would either take an overriding order from Ray for them to not detain Locke, or some kind of diversion which would probably backfire and get them in even more trouble.

And if they did manage to get into Daniel's room, they couldn't guarantee that he'd even talk to them. He hadn't been so forthcoming at Kaylee's house. Their best chance of answers was Kaylee, if they could get in her room. Or if they found someone else who already had access.

"What about Ray?" Locke shifted in his seat so that he faced her better. "Or even Mikio. Do you think either of them could get in Kaylee's room and ask her about the names on the list she gave us? If we know how they're linked, we might be able to find out who is messing with our phones and who twisted the bomb threat to make it look like it was me."

Alana's eyes widened. "What if it was Ray who did it?"

Alana didn't want to believe her brother might be working against them—working with criminals who might want to kill the president. That would go against everything she'd thought she knew about him. But her experience of her brother was a relationship from years ago.

"Maybe I'm just being overly cautious, but it's not a completely crazy idea given the couple of days we've had."

Ray could be deliberately sabotaging their attempts to figure this out. Or, just as easily, drawing added attention to them to throw the Secret Service off the scent of what was really going on.

The reality was that she knew little about what kind of man he was now. Ray could have a wife. Or a girlfriend. Lots of men didn't wear their wedding rings these days. He could have a child at home. Alana could have a niece or nephew she didn't even know about. Just as plausibly, Ray could have gotten involved with something out of his depth. His sympathies could have changed, and he could have crossed a professional line somewhere on the path of his career the last few years and she'd never have known about the slip.

She didn't want to believe it, but that didn't mean it wasn't possible. Good people did bad things and made wrong choices all the time.

Locke's face had softened. Alana didn't need to see that. It was already way too weird being with him like this. Nothing had happened, but it was obvious with how free he was in touching her—whenever he thought she might need a squeeze of her hand to remember he was right there—that something had changed. And she couldn't deny that Locke had become more than a boss to her these last couple of days.

It was clear he'd only been protecting her by asking her if she wanted to leave. She loved that he'd given her the choice. But there was no way she would leave her colleague—her friend—in the middle of this. She wouldn't figure it out alone, and neither could he. Their best chance of working out what was going on was to stick together.

"I'll try calling him again." It was the only way they'd know. But in her heart she knew her brother was a good man. If he'd crossed a line, then it would be for a good reason. Though she prayed he'd never have to face that. Alana was willing to go as far as praying to a God Locke was sure existed, especially if it might save her brother.

She clicked on his contact on her phone, now that she had his number again. It rang but cut off before the first ring could finish and then beeped at her. "It's not working." She sighed. "We could go to the hospital and call from there."

"That might be our best option. If we can't call Ray, then we can't call Mikio and we can't call for help, either. Someone is hindering our progress, but unless we get where we're going, we won't make any headway on this case."

Alana pressed her lips together. Locke didn't need to know how scared she was. He was already worried enough—even if he'd told her he had *faith*. Whoever was behind this whole thing had tried to kill her, then they'd tried to kill both of them and a restaurant full of cops. Was it because of a plot to kill the president? It made no sense, even if that was right. Why would someone target only them and not all the Secret Service agents, or even all the ones who had come early on the advance team? There were less obvious ways to attempt to kill the president—ones that didn't involve giving away the fact you were up to something before POTUS even arrived on the Big Island.

"What if we go back to the hotel and meet up with Director Matthews?"

Locke pulled out into traffic, apparently done sitting in one spot. "We can explain to William what happened and get some help with our phones."

Alana nodded. "We don't have to do this alone—just the two of us, I mean. We have a team."

"I'm glad you said that. It's what you've been taught, and I should've remembered it as well. Until it's clear they're the enemy—which would be crazy—we have to still work on the basis that the Secret Service are our friends. It's what our training tells us."

"So we're going back to the hotel?"

He nodded. "It's a good idea. We need more intel on Brian Wells, and we need to know if the police turned up anything on the BOLO yet. The Secret Service can hold us if necessary until the local police—"

"You mean Ray."

He shrugged. "Until they're satisfied we're not the enemy."

Alana looked out the window. The sun had begun its evening trek down to the horizon, a sight she had missed in DC nearly every day she'd been there. Now she couldn't enjoy it because of this cloud over their heads. She couldn't even surf because of the wound on her abdomen. Confusion, deception—she had no idea what to make of it all. Or how Ray could possibly believe that Locke was the kind of man who would betray the oath he'd taken to protect the president.

But maybe he didn't believe it. And maybe that was why he'd warned Locke that he was coming to arrest him. Ray could have simply told him as a courtesy, or to convey he was doing his duty but under protest. He'd catch flack for that when it came out, but if Ray had done it because he didn't want to arrest Locke, she was grateful.

She trusted Locke, and that should be enough for her brother to know that something had gone wrong— that someone had twisted his words to implicate him. Maybe they'd even doctored the 9-1-1 recording the way his emails had been altered.

Alana realized that she was more mad than scared. With only a single father after her mother had died, she'd been taught that crying was for sissies. Her dad had been great, so long as everyone's emotions were in check. Kaylee had possessed enough emotion for the two of them, so Alana had held hers close. Especially after her accident. She hadn't been allowed to get upset, but she'd been allowed to get mad.

Anger had a purpose—it could be channeled, and she was going to use it now. She needed to do exactly what her father had taught her. Exactly what the Secret Service had trained her to do: take those skills, find Brian Wells and figure out who was messing with her life and Locke's career.

Alana tapped her phone against her leg.

"I can hear your brain ticking from all the way over here."

Alana shut her eyes and pictured Brian Wells's home. The papers. The mail she'd leafed through. The TV. The beat-up coffee table. He was an aging sniper. He hunted game. He could be in the woods and they'd never find him. He probably knew every inch of this land. But he wasn't off the grid. Brian Wells had come into town to shoot up the restaurant. Which meant he might even still be in town.

Which meant he needed somewhere to sleep while he was here.

"Like the homeless shelter."

"What's that?"

"Take the next exit." She paused. "I know we were supposed to go to the hotel, but this could be a real lead. Can we check it out and then contact the team after?"

Locke took the turn. "They probably have a phone we can use to tell the team what's happening."

Alana directed him through an older part of town where a lot of homeless who weren't beach dwellers gravitated. Restaurants that handed out food after hours. A clinic that took cash to treat people with no insurance—and sometimes no ID. "Right here."

She pointed to an open space then looked at Locke. "If we had more time, I'd suggest a change of clothes so we'd blend in, but we'll have to do."

The Sunshine Residence opened its doors every day to serve meals and closed them every night with the hundreds of beds they had full. "Find a picture of Brian Wells on your iPad and let's go show it around. If God really is in the business of answering prayers, then we'll find him. Or we'll find someone who's seen Wells, and get a better idea of where he's hiding out."

"He is." Locke grabbed his iPad, and they crossed the street to the run-down building that had been repainted recently but not repaired. They had some money, but not enough to put to rights what was really wrong.

The front desk was manned by an older gentleman in a biker vest with a name tag that read Wolf. His stringy gray hair was tied back, and when he saw them enter, his craggy face lifted. "Can I help you folks?"

They showed him their badges and then the photo of Brian Wells. When the man had gotten over his surprise at being confronted by two Secret Service agents—they got that a lot—he pointed an arthritic finger to a set of double doors. "Sure, he's in there eating with the rest of our guests."

TWELVE

The dining hall was full of people. In one quick over-view, Locke spotted a dozen women and a few children, but generally it was men who were sitting in rows eating something that smelled like chili made out of the ham that came in cans. He strode down the aisles, laid out like a school cafeteria. He didn't draw his weapon and wouldn't until it became necessary.

The serving window and the last few people getting the scrapings from the giant pots were to his left. At the far left corner was a hall, which the desk guy had told him was where the bathrooms and an exit were located. He scanned every face as he passed, but the noise level in the room was decreasing as people took in the two suited agents clearly searching for someone. They stuck out here, just like they did in most of Hawaii. But these people were in a bad season, out of work, or homeless. Many were veterans, if the jackets and patches and tattoos were anything to go by.

If Brian Wells had been eating earlier, he might've finished and left—or gone upstairs to a room where he would spend the night. They were likely going to have to search the whole building, which, with no additional manpower to help, was going to take a while. And it would give Wells plenty of opportunity to give them the slip.

A burly man at Locke's ten o'clock one row over threw down his spoon and stood. He wiped his hands on a napkin and then tossed it onto his tray.

Before the man could make a move, Locke lifted one hand and strode down the aisle past the guy. "I'm not here for you. I don't want any trouble, I'm just looking for someone." He surveyed the ends of the rows of diners. No one moved. No one spoke except a couple of kids in the corner wrestling.

"I don't see him." Alana's voice was softer and had that same lilt the locals spoke with. She probably didn't hear it, and likewise didn't know it served to soften the room to the two outsiders. Hawaiians had a slang word for mainlanders, but Locke didn't remember it until someone muttered it under their breath.

"I don't see him, either." Locke scanned the room one more time.

A door swished, and a man emerged at the end of the hall. Damp hands. Brian Wells had been in the bathroom.

He took in the two agents in suits and froze for a second.

"We just want to talk."

Brian swung around and dashed down the hallway. Locke tore after him and reached the mouth of the hall with Alana on his heels. Brian hit the bar on the door at the far end and raced out the fire exit.

The back alley smelled like the trash that overflowed from a Dumpster pushed against one side of the stucco building. Locke could feel the sweat accumulate as he ran after the former sniper. But they were catching up to the older man with the noticeable limp. The street at the end of the alley was busy, two lanes in both directions and a steady stream of buses and cars that made up the evening rush hour. Brian turned the corner.

A couple of teens stepped off the curb and crossed in front of the alley.

Locke skidded around the corner and sidestepped a stroller pushed by a mom in workout gear. "Sorry."

He ran on, but the crowd of people on the sidewalk was significant. When he hit the next intersection, he stopped and scanned in every direction as he puffed out each breath. "We lost him."

Alana stopped beside him. "Gone?"

He nodded.

She shook her head and blew out her own fast breaths. "I can't believe he was right there. That was unreal."

"But Wells slipped through our fingers, and we lost the chance to find out what he's tied up in."

There were still leads to be found here, though. The people Brian Wells had been living and eating with had to know something about him. No one lived in a vacuum, or at least very few people were able to sustain it. There had to be someone back at the shelter who knew where he'd been going or who he associated with.

Alana brushed away unruly hair that had escaped her ponytail and set her hands on her hips. "Let's go back and talk to the guy on the desk."

Locke nodded. "That's exactly what I was thinking."

They circled the building instead of going back through the dining room and disturbing all the people in there again. Locke held the door for Alana, and they strode to the man with the name tag that said Wolf. His desk was surrounded by a crowd of people complaining about the "suits."

Wolf yelled over their talking. "Enough!" He motioned to Locke and Alana with his chin and everyone skedaddled. "Right. Suppose you want to know what I know?"

Locke nearly smiled. Apparently Wolf knew the drill, which made him wonder what interaction he'd had with the law before. "That would be nice."

The man sniffed. "Wells has been here about four days, but he does that every few months. Sleeps. Eats. Rest of the time he's gone. Don't know where, never seen him talk to anyone."

"Anything else?"

He stared at Locke, as though it was an expedient method of assessing the character of a man. "Fine. There was this one guy." Wolf looked aside. "It was a few weeks, maybe two months ago. Dressed like you two."

"Alone?"

The man nodded. "Looking for Brian, just like you."

Locke felt Alana move closer to him to hear the man's quietly spoken words. Locke said, "He asked for Brian?"

"Had one of the guys get Brian from the bunk room. Saw him speak to the guy."

"Do you have surveillance?" Alana's question was hopeful. When the man shook his head, she got out her phone and pulled up the BOLO information. She showed him a picture of Daniel Kaiko. "This him?"

"No, because that guy's local. And yakuza aren't welcome here." The man frowned. "Besides, the guy was a mainlander."

"You're sure?" Locke said. He showed Wolf a picture of Zane Franks.

"Nope. Not him either."

Alana shot Locke a side glance at the same time Wolf continued, "Suit, but he looked comfortable in it. I asked Brian what it was about. He said the guy offered him a job. Never said if he took it, though. But it looked like they made plans to meet up later. He took the man's card."

If they could get ahold of that card, say, from Brian Wells's belongings, they could see who it was. Would the instigator of a plot to put the president in danger really give out his business card? Not likely, but it was a possible lead.

"Any way we can see his belongings? He might've left that card behind."

"No way. I don't run that kind of business here. You might be cops or whatnot, but people have a right to privacy."

Locke shot the man a look that told him everything he was feeling about Wolf hindering their investigation. "A description then, at least?"

The man nodded and gave them some basic info that Alana jotted down. Blond, graying hair. Suit, but it became clear Wolf didn't know the difference between tailored and off-the-rack. The man could have been a Secret Service agent just as he could have been anyone off the street with one nice outfit. They would probably never know who had pulled Brian Wells into this.

Alana shot Wolf a smile. "Thank you for your help. We're sorry for the disturbance." She started to walk away.

"One second," Locke said to her. He turned to the man. "Can I use your phone? Ours aren't working."

The man handed Locke the handset and turned the phone so he could see the numbers. Locke called Agent Carlsen, who was on their team, and updated him.

"That's a relief," Carlsen said. "We were worried about you. Director Matthews told everyone that if you called in, we're supposed to get your location and come pick you up."

Locke figured as much. "We're headed back to the hotel now to meet up with you all." They were so close to getting Wells, Locke didn't want to waste any more time. Especially not when he didn't totally trust William. But they needed to regroup. And rest.

"The president is headed to a desert with the governor right now, and we've doubled up on his detail because of whatever's going on with you. But I'll tell Director Matthews what you said."

"Thanks, Carlsen. And make sure you call intelligence when you get a minute. Ask them about their progress looking into my emails, okay?"

"Got it."

Locke hung up. Alana led the way outside, back to the car.

They needed a win on something, with the police thinking he was a traitor and his own people unable to contact him. Locke didn't know what he would do if even one Secret Service agent doubted the oath that he'd made. He would never earn back the loss of trust and respect, and that was essential in this business.

Right now, all he had were God and Alana on his side.

And that was enough to see him through.

She turned to Locke. "It was a good lead. We know where Brian Wells has been sleeping and where he eats. That's something."

"You're right. Going to the homeless shelter was a great idea." He pulled out his phone. "Still no signal.

It can't be proximity. People around us have working phones. If someone is messing with them, it's targeted at ours specifically, and it started after I called intelligence and found out someone messed with my reports."

"So we're headed to the hotel now to check in with Director Matthews? He can help us clear up the confusion with the police." She paused. "With Ray."

He almost looked nervous. Alana set her hand on his shoulder. "I'm going to stick by you, no matter what. We haven't done anything to cast suspicion on us. If this is an attempt to discredit you, there's no way it's going to stick. No way."

"Thank you. I need your confidence in me."

He was a good man who didn't deserve to have his career trashed by lies. Alana didn't want to work in a place that would allow that kind of thing to happen. Federal agency or not, they were held to a high standard, and she believed in it. But not at the expense of someone's life. Wrongs were committed all the time, but it was injustice she just couldn't abide.

She knew what it was like to have a dream. Surfing had been the driving force behind her entire life. Then one day that dream was dead and she'd been forced to salvage a new dream from the wreckage of the one she'd had.

He drove this time, while Alana tried both phones and messaging on the iPad. Email didn't work, either. A signal jammer would have to have been placed in the car to block a signal where they were. If they moved any significant distance from it, things would begin to work again. But this seemed different. No matter where they were, their phones were spotty.

It wasn't a foolproof method of segregating them from their team—more like an annoyance. So why would someone be doing this to them? It wasn't a good tactic if it was a plan that depended on them being out of contact.

Their phones hadn't worked right since after Locke had found out about his reports being falsified. And they hadn't worked when they were away from the car. Maybe the jammer was on one of them...or was it the phones and Locke's iPad themselves and it had nothing to do with proximity.

Alana just couldn't figure out what the reason was. Let alone who was behind it.

Locke pulled onto the freeway. A minute later they were surrounded by three black SUVs.

"Government plates?"

Alana glanced around, twisting in her seat to see. "Hawaiian, it looks like, but they could be rentals."

The three vehicles boxed them in. At the next exit, they were forced to get off the freeway or get hit. Locke drove in the center of the huddle, which forced him to turn onto a side street. The SUVs sped up and one turned in front of him.

Locke screeched to a halt, locking both of their seat belts.

Armed yakuza soldiers jumped out and surrounded them.

THIRTEEN

When Mikio Adachi emerged from the rear of the vehicle to their left, Alana cracked her door. "Hold up." Locke didn't want her to get out before he did. Neither of them had body armor, and these men had automatic weapons. If he thought it would help and not wind up a bloodbath, he might've seen if his phone worked and called the police.

Except it was more likely he'd end up the one arrested, not these yakuza gunmen. Better than being dead, though.

Mikio stood beside his vehicle inside the circle of protection provided by his men. His sunglasses hid his eyes, but from what Locke could see of his face the man wore a neutral expression. He didn't move. Locke and Alana waited. After a minute, Mikio reached into his pants pocket and pulled out a cell phone.

"Daniel Kaiko's phone."

A peace offering. "Fine," Locke said, "but we do this slow and careful. I do not want the situation to erupt just because someone made a miscalculation and we end up with one of these itchy triggers taking out a bystander."

The streets were sparse, but people could come upon

them at any moment. He didn't want anyone getting caught in the crossfire.

Alana nodded. "Slow and careful." She pushed her door open wider.

Locke got out on his side and made sure it was clear to all of these men that he would go out protecting her if that was what it took. God had given him these protective instincts for a reason—and if that reason was to take care of Alana, then he was good with it. Whether it was in the normal course of his job or because their relationship had moved in that direction didn't matter. Either was good.

Locke caught her gaze as she rounded the hood of the car and then faced forward to keep watch on each of the gunmen. But it wasn't the scene that eclipsed his thoughts. Instead, what he couldn't help thinking was that he *wanted* more than just a work relationship with her. Alana meant something to him, something important he wanted to explore.

Right now was the wrong time for him to have realized it, but it was what it was. He couldn't help the timing. *God, get us through this without anyone getting hurt. Help us get the answers we so desperately need.*

Alana stepped forward slowly. Mikio did the same.

Mikio's eyes flashed. "Scared of me now?"

"You forced us off the road, and now your armed guards are pointing machine guns at us." Alana's tone matched what Locke felt. She'd considered this man a friend at one point in her life, but she was as done with his shenanigans as Locke. She said, "How are those the actions of someone intent on portraying the fact they're at all trustworthy?"

Mikio nodded, the epitome of grace. He almost could

have been a Japanese state leader. Except he'd need more gray hair. "My apologies."

"If you'll grant me the phone, Director Locke and I will be leaving now."

Mikio smiled. "Of course." He held the phone out. Alana reached for it, but at the last second he pulled it back. "Oh, just one more thing first."

Games. Locke hated games, and he hated that this man was intent on playing them with him and Alana. Mikio was counting on Alana's sympathies and his ties to her sister. Mikio didn't know the kind of woman Alana had become since he'd known her years ago.

One of Mikio's men actually snickered. Locke wasn't going to stand for his partner being taken for a fool. He strode forward and stopped, facing Mikio, his shoulder in front of Alana. He drew his weapon. "Want me to arrest you and take the phone that way? Because I will."

Mikio lifted his free hand, palm out. "Perhaps I will rescind my offer. Or simply neglect to tell you the passcode."

"Daniel Kaiko is in police custody." His phone could potentially provide them with intel they needed—intel they had no access to otherwise. But Mikio didn't need to know that; he could go on believing they considered Daniel a done part of this.

"Then you don't require the phone?"

Alana said, "Neither do you. Since I'm guessing you went through it already and deleted anything… incriminating."

Mikio smiled. There was an edge to him, but while he was every inch the yakuza boss here, Locke could also see how—back in the day—he'd been just another kid at school. He still had that youthful air, like he could shuck the yakuza boss skin he wore at any time. Locke hoped that was what drew Kaylee to him and not his dangerous side. The woman needed someone safe, just like Alana did, not a guy who was going to put her at risk even more.

And yeah, Alana's sister's relationship status wasn't really his business, but he cared about Alana, so why wouldn't he care about her sister, as well? He had sisters, and if one of them were dating a gangster he'd for sure have something to say about it.

"I protect what's mine."

Locke studied his face. "What does that mean?"

"Kaylee is in danger."

"Yesterday when she'd stood you up, you were ready to call it quits and move on. Why the sudden change of heart? Find something in Daniel's phone?"

"I have reason to believe Kaylee is in danger. If I give you the phone, I want your guarantee Kaylee will be protected."

Alana said, "Who is she in danger from? Daniel?"

Locke waited for the answer. It made sense if Mikio had gone through the phone. When the yakuza boss said nothing, Locke answered, "I'm guessing yes. I just don't see how you think we can help. I doubt the cops will let us in, even if we wanted to do you this favor."

"You will, or you don't get the phone." Mikio's stare hardened. "Kaylee is in danger, and it's happening tonight."

Alana shrugged one shoulder. "How are you so sure?"

"Because *I am*." Mikio ran a hand through his hair and down his face. "Why are you still standing here when I've told you that she's in danger? Don't you care about your sister?"

Locke didn't need Alana to answer that. He said, "Sorry, we don't jump when you tell us to."

Locke wasn't opposed to watching out for Kaylee, especially if it got them a step closer to whoever was behind this whole thing. Still. "But what about Ray? He's probably got the whole police force on the warpath, convinced the bomb threat against the president was my doing. So how do we convince him we're at the hospital to protect Kaylee when he wants to arrest me?"

"Bomb threat?" When Locke nodded, Mikio said, "I wondered what all the fuss was about. They shut the whole block down and rushed the president out the back."

Alana blew out a breath. Even though Agent Carlsen had told them POTUS was fine, it was still a relief to hear that steps had been taken.

"What about Ray?" Mikio still hadn't answered Locke's question.

"You let me worry about Ray and his orders." Mikio apparently wasn't too bothered about the rest of the police force. "You protect Kaylee. The cops won't let me in there, especially not with the kind of firepower Kaylee needs to keep her safe."

"From who?" Locke wanted an answer. "Is someone coming to hurt her?"

"To kill her." Mikio tossed Locke the phone. "I have what I need. But if anything happens to Kaylee, that's on *you*."

"You're going to threaten federal agents? We're supposed to be protecting the president and you want us doing a favor for you?"

Mikio stepped back and then started to walk to his vehicle. "Like I said, I'll take care of Ray. Don't worry about the cops, but if something happens to her, that's on you. And I don't take my promises lightly."

"I don't like this at all." But he didn't stop; Locke just kept moving through the underground parking garage at the hospital.

"Do we have a choice?" Alana followed Locke, scanning the garage as they made their way to the door. Inside the stairwell they headed up two floors to the lobby. If Kaylee was truly in danger, what else could they do but protect her? They could contact the Secret Service from a hospital phone.

Locke went up three steps and pointed to the desk. "Over there."

He strode up to the front desk and flashed his badge but didn't give them his name. Hopefully the police didn't have a BOLO out that had been disseminated to hospital staff with their pictures on it. That was the last thing they needed.

"I need to use your phone." He had two cell phones on him, but theirs weren't working and he wasn't about to use Daniel Kaiko's phone. Technically it was evidence in whatever case this was, though they had to figure out how to get it turned over to the police without getting arrested in the process.

She watched his fingers as he dialed. He was calling Director Matthews. They'd talked about it in the car, worked out their plan to get their team over to the hospital—at least whoever wasn't actively protecting the president. POTUS came before their problems, every time. There was no other way it was going to go.

But would William listen, or would he dismiss Locke's concern over his problem with Ray and the rest of law enforcement the way Locke had told her he'd done after Beatrice was killed?

"It's Locke." He paused. Alana stepped closer and Locke tilted the phone so she could hear, as well.

"…the situation. Where are you?"

"We're at the hospital."

"Once I have the president secure to my satisfaction I'll be there. Do not go anywhere, and do not move from that position."

"Copy that," Locke said.

"What is wrong with your phones? Agent Carlsen said you were having trouble, and intel told him the GPS has been spotty all night, popping up all over the place. We've been trying to find both of you."

"We think someone is messing with them," Locke said. "We've been trying to call in from our phones. And we did call 9-1-1 from a pharmacy clerk's cell phone, and called the police—specifically Sergeant Ray Preston—from Zane Franks's house."

William said, "We got the president secured, but the word from the police came in that you were the one threatening to bomb him tonight. No one believed it, but we have POTUS to cover."

"Good. Thank you for believing me, and tell the team I said thanks, as well." Locke blew out a breath.

Alana looked up, and they shared a relieved smile. There was no way the team could believe that suddenly Locke had turned against them, but it felt good to know for sure that they'd never doubted Locke was on their side.

Locke continued, "So we'll hang here and wait for you. But we're going upstairs to make sure Kaylee Preston is secure. If there's an active threat, we have to be prepared to defend her. She may be the only one with answers as to what's going on."

"Copy that. See you soon."

Locke hung up. The receptionist shot him a look and took the phone back. He led Alana back over to the stairwell. "Not the elevator?"

Locke shook his head. "The cops will be watching it. With the stairs we can keep an eye out and emerge when we want to. If more officers are headed here to arrest me I don't want the cops who are supposed to be watching Kaylee to get distracted and lose focus because we're here."

"Okay. Isn't William going to call the cops and tell them everything is fine?"

"Sure, but it'll take time for that information to disseminate down the ranks."

They went up to the eighth floor, and Locke peered through the slit window in the door. Alana hung back, waiting for him to give the go-ahead. Mikio's words replayed in her head over and over. If he cared so much, why not face the police and protect Kaylee himself? She could understand him not wanting the hassle, but if he truly cared for Kaylee, he would find a way to help her. He would make it so the police had no reason to stop him, which probably meant going legit or leaving the yakuza altogether.

Mikio couldn't have it both ways, and if her sister would actually talk to her, Alana wanted to know how Kaylee felt about that.

All she wanted was peace with her sister, not the strife that was between them right now. But Alana couldn't even do that when her sister wouldn't let her in. How could they protect Kaylee when she wouldn't let them visit, even if they could get past the police officer stationed outside?

"Everything looks quiet." Locke turned back. He frowned. "You okay?"

Alana sighed. "I'm just trying to figure out why Mikio told us to come here." She paused. "He could have called Ray, told him to beef up Kaylee's security. But he didn't—he bargained with us."

Locke's face softened. "I know you're worried about her, but there's a cop outside her room and Daniel has his own guard. He isn't going anywhere."

Alana's stomach churned. "Wells is a sniper. He could shoot Kaylee through the window."

"So we search the surrounding rooftops, look for a sniper."

"But he could shoot her in one second. We would be too late, and unable to stop him."

"So we get her moved to another room." She could see the ideas ticking behind his eyes. "The cops already think I'm trying to kill the president." He lifted Daniel's phone. "How about we make them think I'm trying to kill Kaylee, as well?"

He really wanted to do that? She didn't detect a sardonic tone to his voice, but wasn't sure if he was being facetious or not. "Daniel's phone works?"

He nodded. "There's a signal, so I can try."

"That means the problem with our phones isn't local to us. It's coming from somewhere else, directed specifically at our phones."

"So it's a techie-type person, or someone who paid a hacker or an employee at our carrier company?" Locke didn't look pleased. "Someone who knows how to get past the extra security measures the Secret Service puts in."

She nodded. It might come back to bite them, but they needed results. Fast.

"Okay, I'll call in the threat. We need Kaylee moved to another room." Locke got into the phone. He spoke to someone, asking for the homicide department because he wanted to report a homicide that was about to happen. Alana would have rolled her eyes at his dour tone if this wasn't a serious situation. At least he wasn't tying up the line with a 9-1-1 dispatcher.

When he hung up, they waited. Alana paced the landing between the concrete stairs that led down to the floor below and up to the floor above. The air-conditioning chilled her so that goose bumps prickled her skin. Alana rubbed her arms, not really sure what they were waiting for. A rush of security personnel, or an announcement. Something like that.

Locke touched her elbow, and she stilled. He moved closer. "Everything's going to be okay. All right?"

She nodded, but she didn't believe it. Locke couldn't control what was happening. If he could, Ray wouldn't be out to arrest him.

Locke touched her cheek. His hand was warm, far warmer than she was. Alana moved closer, into his heat. He smiled down at her, and she tried to return it. Things weren't okay—far from it, actually. Why wasn't he freaking out? Locke touched her other cheek. "Alana."

His face descended, and it dawned on her that he was going to kiss her.

"Code gray. Security to the tenth floor." A crackly voice came over the loudspeaker in the ceiling. "This is a lockdown. Code gray. Please do not leave your rooms. We have an escaped prisoner loose in the hospital."

FOURTEEN

Alana pulled away. An escaped prisoner? "Could it be Daniel?"

Locke looked disappointed, though probably not about Daniel Kaiko being loose in the hospital. Part of her was pleased, but there wasn't enough time to dwell on what that kiss might have been like if it had actually happened.

She turned to the window and looked out into the hall. The police officer outside Kaylee's room was on the phone, pacing and paying no attention to what was going on around him. Her sister was exposed! The officer was going to fail in his duties now, when it might matter most.

"We should go and find out what happened," Locke said. "See if we can help. I'm sure they need as many people as possible to find whoever it is that has escaped."

"This could all be an elaborate ruse. Mikio might have brought us here because his intention all along was for Daniel to break out. He's probably going to blame it on us so it looks like we had something to do with it."

"Why?" Locke shrugged. "That would leave Kaylee exposed."

"And Daniel is out. Maybe Mikio is coming here to get her in the middle of the confusion."

"You think he's going to abduct her while everyone is searching for Daniel?"

Alana didn't say anything. It was plain that Locke didn't think Mikio would try to do that. But the yakuza boss was certainly cunning enough to create a scenario wherein he got exactly what he wanted. He'd been like that his whole life, and Alana had seen him do it before—though that time it had been about passing history and staying on the football team.

Locke sighed. "You go out there. Stay with Kaylee, maybe get her moved to a different room. But keep her safe. I'll go help the cops and security search for Daniel. It isn't like there's much else we can do when the hospital is on lockdown."

"Okay." She didn't like splitting up, but it would be for the best.

Locke pulled her to him, and they hugged.

"Thanks."

Locke's eyes widened for a second, then he smiled at her and said, "Be careful." He went up the first step.

"You, too." Alana pulled the door open and stepped into the busy hallway. Rooms were locked, the desk unmanned. The cop outside Kaylee's door was one of only a couple of people still in the hall and not in a room.

"Hold up." He lifted one hand, the other on his gun, which he unclipped.

Alana motioned to the badge on the chain around her neck. "Do I look like an escaped prisoner to you?" The more she acted the part of the confident Secret Service agent, the more it was believed. No one saw her as legit when she was unsure of herself or what she should be doing. "Kaylee Preston is my sister, and I'd like to personally make sure she is secured."

"You're Alana Preston." The cop pressed his thin lips together. "The sergeant said you might come by."

"Whatever Ray told you, those are your orders. But there's an escaped prisoner loose in this hospital, and I'm going to make sure my sister is secure."

"Fine."

"I want her moved to another room."

"Not fine." The cop shook his head in a jerky motion. "Everyone stays in their rooms. It's procedure, or did you not hear the announcement?"

"I'll think on it."

She would more than think about moving her sister. Alana moved to the door of Kaylee's room. She was going to make a plan that got her sister to a different room, and she couldn't do that without bringing her out into the hall. Alana didn't bother knocking. When she let herself in, Kaylee was sitting up, the remote in her hand and her eyes on the TV, which was playing local news. Good, that meant Kaylee was awake enough they could move her without Alana having to find out how much her sister weighed.

Kaylee grimaced, not turning her attention from the TV. "Figures you'd sneak in eventually."

"I'm not sneaking. If Daniel has escaped, I don't want him coming anywhere near you." Alana glanced at the window. The blinds were closed. Could Brian Wells have a heat scope to shoot through to the person on the bed? Could Alana risk her sister's life in the process of finding out whether he was better than she'd anticipated?

Alana crossed and closed the heavy drapes as well,

just in case it made a difference. She went back to the door and looked out into the hall. "Good. Let's go."

Kaylee lifted her hands. "Go where?" Her medical bracelet slid down her slender wrist. Why did she seem so fragile? She was a grown woman who had withstood so much of what Alana had, just at a younger age.

"A different room." Alana strode to her sister. "There's no wheelchair in here, so you'll have to walk."

Kaylee had one bandage taped to her left temple and another wrapped around her wrist. Alana tried not to look overlong at either while she pulled the blankets back. She reached for her sister's feet.

"Hey." Kaylee pulled her legs into her body. "I'm cold. Put the blanket back on."

"Cold is better than dead. Let's move." Alana waved her sister off the bed. "We need to be elsewhere when Brian Wells opens fire on your room from a rooftop and sniper rounds start flying through that window." She pointed at the drapes, her breath coming fast.

Kaylee frowned but thankfully swung her legs over the side of the bed. She looked at Alana like she'd grown two heads. "Help me out. I'm kinda shaky still."

Alana pulled her sister's arm across her shoulders and took the bulk of Kaylee's weight. She walked her sister down to the next room, across the hall. She ignored the blustering cop. Protection details changed on a dime all the time. He needed to be more flexible.

She settled her on the bed, which had a fitted sheet and no blankets. Alana went back and got the pillow and covers, tucking them around her sister.

Kaylee leaned back against the pillow. "The TV had better work. That's all I'm saying."

"If it doesn't, we'll just have to talk instead."

"About what?"

"Oh, I don't know. How about those four names you gave me? Why your business card was at Brian Wells's house. Why Daniel Kaiko was questioning you. Or maybe why he tried to kill me—which Locke thinks was because Daniel might've mistaken me for you."

"Yes, Locke." Kaylee fingered the remote but didn't try to turn the TV on. "He's cute. Are you seeing each other?"

"What? No." Alana halted before she could step back. Kaylee would know what retreat meant.

Her sister laughed. "You like him. He likes you, too. Who wouldn't?" There was an edge of bitterness in her voice.

"What is that supposed to mean?"

Kaylee shrugged and looked away. "Don't pretend you want to know what I think. Or that you care."

"Of course I care. How can you say that?" The woman gave her whiplash. Last time her sister hadn't even let her in the room, and now she'd done what Alana asked. For a minute Kaylee had talked to her like they were friends and not estranged, and now she'd flipped back to guarded. Alana couldn't figure her out at all. "I don't understand you. How could I when you screamed at me to get out of your life? Well, guess what, I did it. And now you're acting like I'm the one who wronged *you*."

The door opened. "Kaylee?" It was Ray.

"In here." Kaylee didn't waste time getting Ray in the room to act as a buffer.

Ray strode in, mouth open to say something when the window blew out. Glass sprayed across the room and tufts of curtain flew through the air.

Sniper.

How had he found them across the hall?

* * *

Locke scanned the room, then moved to the next door and opened it. A janitor's closet. He depressed the button on the radio the security staff had given him and held it to his mouth. "Ninth floor west is clear."

The next door was the stairwell. This entire floor was nothing but scared oncology patients who didn't need this disruption to their already difficult lives. He'd prayed for each of them as he searched the floor, just as he prayed for Alana to be safe and for her sister to open up to her. As far as he could see, it would take God's intervention to get the two stubborn women to find a place where they could actually dialogue. It seemed like all Alana's family did was fall back into old hurts and get defensive. All three of them needed to forgive each other and move on or they'd never work it out.

The stairwell was clear. Locke went up to join the search on the tenth floor. He doubted Daniel would have gone up there—and it was Daniel who'd escaped, killing his police guards in the process. Locke figured the former SEAL would more likely head for the nearest exit, but this was what the head of security had told him to do. Locke had his part to play, and if everyone did their jobs, then every inch of this hospital would be searched and Daniel Kaiko would be found.

Locke put his back to the wall, then leaned forward and glanced through the window. Someone was coming. The door to the stairs opened, and a man in hospital scrubs stepped in. A surgical mask covered his mouth and nose, partly obscuring his features. But it was Daniel Kaiko.

Locke waited until he'd cleared the door. "Hands up."

Daniel swung around, a scalpel in his hand.

Locke deflected the scalpel with a sideswipe to Daniel's forearm. He whipped the gun back and slammed it into Daniel's shoulder right where he'd shot the former SEAL. He wasn't going to shoot the man now, not when it was gun versus knife. Locke had far more honor than that, and they'd never get any answers from the man if he was dead.

Daniel cried out, and Locke grabbed his shoulders. He slammed his knee into the man's face. Daniel whipped out again with the knife. It glanced off Locke's thigh.

He hissed and renewed his fight. They grappled. Daniel punched Locke, and the scalpel nicked his ear. His vision blurred. A sharp pain slit the vest he wore on his left side, by his ribs.

Locke grabbed Daniel's arm and slammed it against the wall over and over until Daniel dropped the knife. His breath heaved in his chest, every intake like fire. Daniel shifted behind Locke and punched his kidney. Locke went down to one knee as pain ricocheted through his abdomen. He tackled Daniel's legs and they fell down the stairs, rolling so Locke hit twice before he ended up on Daniel on the landing between floors. The phones in his pocket cracked—one or both of them.

The former SEAL rolled and slammed Locke's head on the concrete. Light spilled through the window, sparking stars through his vision. Daniel pulled back his arm, fist balled to punch Locke. But he never did.

Daniel was hauled off Locke, and William pinned him to the wall. "Enough." He turned Daniel so his face was pressed against the wall and cuffed his hands behind his back. Then he pushed the man so that he sat on the stairs. William pulled his gun. "Don't move."

Locke blew out a breath and climbed to his feet, wincing when the cut on his leg pulled open. Now he knew how Alana felt. He looked down. Blood soaked his pant leg. "Pretty handy with knives, aren't you?"

That was twice Daniel had stabbed someone, along with one attempt on Kaylee that they'd stopped.

Daniel lifted his chin. "What are you talking about? I missed."

"I didn't." Locke held his weapon loose in his hands. The temptation to just shoot this man and end the drama was strong, but he couldn't be the man Alana deserved if he gave in and took the easy way out.

He strode past Daniel up the stairs, ignoring the pain, and found the radio. It wasn't broken. *Thank You.* At least one piece of technology he had was working. "This is Director James Locke. The escaped prisoner has been found. I'm holding him in the stairwell below the ninth floor."

He exhaled, and all the strength he'd felt seemed to seep out with the blood from the cut on his leg. He turned and saw William eyeing him. "Thank you."

The other director shrugged with a tilt of his head.

"Seriously, I appreciate you getting here so fast and helping me out." Locke paused. Daniel didn't need to know he was suddenly exhausted. It was still hard to breathe. Every inhale was like a stabbing pain. Had Daniel broken his rib? "When security gets here, they can take Kaiko off our hands and get him back in police custody."

William nodded. The man was usually more talkative. Maybe seeing Locke in a full-blown fistfight had shaken him. Their work was usually less…strenuous, and though they trained for exigent circumstances, the reality was that most days were routine.

He walked down the stairs, careful to avoid Daniel's reach. The man didn't move, but he could have chosen that minute to renew his fight—if he wanted William to shoot him, that was.

"So who are you working for?" Locke didn't want to wait for the police to question him. Not if he could get some answers now.

When Daniel said nothing, Locke asked, "Who hired you to get rid of Kaylee Preston? What are you supposed to be doing now? Where did you put the bomb schematics you stole from Beatrice when you killed her?"

Locke still didn't get why Daniel had needed to steal them. They would implicate Beatrice, if they were used. Was it all a frame job?

"Should I continue? Because I have more questions, if you'd like. Feel free to pick one and answer it."

Daniel said nothing. His gaze flicked to William and then back to Locke.

William said, "He's probably not going to tell us anything." He sighed. "I don't suppose the cops will be able to break him, either. He was a SEAL, remember. Those guys have all kinds of training to withstand questioning."

Daniel's lips twitched, as though he thought William's comments hilarious.

Did the other director really think Locke was trying to break the SEAL? He didn't think that was possible, since the man had been trained to withstand anything. Locke would settle for any kind of dialogue whatsoever. Otherwise they weren't going to get anywhere.

"Where does Brian Wells fit into this?" Locke didn't

much care what Daniel talked to him about. Anything was fine. "A former sniper and a former SEAL. I can see how you'd have plenty to bond over, both having been navy. But walking away from the yakuza because you don't like Mikio's girlfriend and trying to kill a Secret Service agent you mistook for her sister seems a bit drastic. And more like a mistake than a plan."

Daniel had gotten it wrong. He could see the anger burn in the former SEAL's eyes. Locke was right—he'd mistaken Alana for Kaylee. "But you didn't kill Kaylee in her apartment. I'm guessing you had to take care of her since she was getting too close. Am I right?"

Locke waited. When Daniel didn't give him anything, he opened his mouth to begin a new line of questioning.

The radio crackled and the head of security's voice came through the speaker. "Shots fired! Eighth floor, east wing." It sounded like he was running.

"Alana." Locke breathed her name.

William glanced at him. "Go."

Locke ran.

FIFTEEN

Ray's weight was on her. Beside Alana, Kaylee grunted as his body covered hers, as well. Alana was the Secret Service agent, but of course Ray was going to play big brother and insist on being the one to protect them both. He'd run across the room as soon as the shooting started. Alana hadn't frozen—she'd been about to pull Kaylee from the bed before Ray did it. He got both of them on the ground.

Sniper fire had blown out the window first, then continued. Shot after shot that made the breath flee from her lungs.

How did Brian Wells know they'd moved rooms? It was possible he had some kind of heat-sensing goggles, or a scope with similar technology, as she'd suspected. He could have seen them, but he'd had to have moved positions as they were on the other side of the hospital now. All that trouble and he hadn't killed them? Maybe he was only taunting them.

She rolled and looked up. Dust in the air. Holes in the wall. The sound was like a low pop. How far away was the man? "He isn't going for accuracy." Just like the restaurant.

"If he was," Ray grunted, "we'd be dead."

"Move so I can get to my phone." Maybe it would actually work this time.

Ray didn't look happy. "Not sure who you're gonna call. Pretty sure the whole hospital knows already."

But where was Locke? Was he safe? Alana needed to make sure. She needed to check in with the man she'd had that moment with on the stairs before he'd gone to find Daniel Kaiko.

"I'm pretty sure your boyfriend's fine. It's us in the line of fire."

Alana sighed. "I can see that."

She wanted to get off the floor. Instead she pushed her brother off her and crawled to the door. He hissed her name, but Alana wasn't going to be a sitting duck when Brian popped off another shot. The cops needed to be searching rooftops for the sniper, but they had to get Kaylee to safety.

She glanced back at her sister, who was pale, with a sheen of perspiration on her face. "You okay?"

Kaylee blinked. She nodded. Alana reached up for the handle.

"Alana?" It was Locke.

"I'm here. Stay out of the line of fire."

They waited, but no more bullets came.

The handle twisted, and he pushed it open, prone as she was on the floor. Alana couldn't help smiling at him.

"Let's get you all out of there."

She nodded and then turned back. "Kaylee, can you crawl to me?"

Ray covered her with his body, keeping himself between their younger sister and the bullets.

Brian Wells hadn't hurt anyone; he'd peppered the

room with rounds and never managed to hit a person. Unlike at the restaurant. Not typical sniper tactics, given they would wait for hours for that perfect shot and didn't usually miss. A sniper's crosshairs were a dangerous place to be—dead before you even knew the shot was coming.

But what was he warning them of—or away from? Two people on the list were dead. The other two were involved in whatever this was. Had Brian Wells simply been creating a diversion to distract them and possibly aid Daniel Kaiko's escape?

That would certainly make sense.

Locke got them all into the hall. "Cops are outside. They'll let me know as soon as they find Wells."

Alana nodded. "Are you okay?" He didn't look so good. Were those cuts?

She wanted to fall into his arms for a hug—or that kiss he'd almost given her earlier—but she had to focus. Locke had been in a fight.

Alana helped her sister to a chair, while Ray's gaze was hard on Locke. Kaylee slumped down and leaned her head against the wall, not nearly as okay as she'd pretended when they'd been talking before Ray came in.

Alana turned to her brother. "What is your problem? We're all fine, and your people will find Wells."

"And Daniel Kaiko is in custody." Locke folded his arms and winced.

Alana glanced between them. Did Locke have a problem with Ray, or was he just matching Ray's demeanor as a defensive reaction? Maybe he intended to fire back for whatever Ray was about to throw at him?

"Both of you stand down." She didn't know what was going on between them but it wasn't nothing. And it was certainly more personal than her brother thinking Locke was a threat to the president. "Ray, maybe you should go…coordinate the search or something."

Ray didn't move.

She sighed. "Locke?"

"We subdued Daniel in the stairwell."

"We?"

"Director Matthews and I." He tore his glare from Ray and looked at her. "I left Daniel with William when I heard the shots."

Because he thought she might be in danger or hurt? "Thank you." Her voice sounded softer than normal, but she couldn't manage to do anything other than melt. He cared about her, and it was a weird feeling considering how long it had been since she'd actually trusted another person with her heart.

His face softened, and he smiled at her.

"And you couldn't have been here? You show up when it's too late and my sister might've been dead?"

Alana spun around. "Ray!" But it was Kaylee's face that snagged her attention. Her younger sister was staring at Locke, at the look on his face. A small smile played on her lips, like it pleased Kaylee to see that he cared about Alana.

Alana focused on her brother. "Ray, are you seriously giving him a hard time about a difference of five minutes?"

"He left you alone."

"He went to look for Daniel."

Ray shrugged. "I left that job in the capable hands of people I trust and came *here* to make sure you and Kaylee were safe."

"And we appreciate that, Ray—"

"Alana."

She ignored Locke trying to interject. "—but when Locke and I agreed to split up, Daniel was loose in the hospital and I wanted to check on Kaylee because Mikio said she might be in danger. Clearly he was right."

"You saw Mikio." Kaylee roused enough to get out of her chair. Apparently talking about Mikio was sufficient motivation.

Ray held out his hand to halt her forward progress but said to Alana, "Don't change the subject."

Kaylee's face fell. Behind Ray's back, Alana's sister pulled the phone from the clip on his belt and sat back down. Ray didn't even notice, and Alana wasn't going to tell him. Kaylee actually looked at Alana like she approved of her for a second.

"You know what, Ray? Back off."

He stepped closer to her, but Locke put a hand on her shoulder. "Both of you need to back off. What's important right now is that everyone is safe. All of you are fine and alive. But this situation is ongoing, and we need to figure out what our next move is going to be."

"Finding Wells." Alana folded her arms.

Locke nodded. "And getting answers from Daniel Kaiko." He shifted to face Ray. "We need a sit-down with Daniel in one of your interrogation rooms."

Ray narrowed his eyes. "I'll have to clear that with my lieutenant first."

Alana said, "Seriously? This is going to help us, maybe even keep the president from getting assassinated, and you're going to stall us because you've decided you don't like Locke?"

"I didn't say I didn't like him," Ray said. "I just disapprove of some of his methods, that's all." He made a face. "Calling in a threat to the president?"

"You need to leave it alone, Ray. Locke was doing his job." It wasn't as though her personal life had anything to do with this, yet that was what it felt like. He was disapproving of her personal choices. "I didn't have a say in who the Secret Service put me with. Now we're just trying to do our best with it."

Locke's mouth worked, and he didn't exactly look happy. What was wrong with what she'd said? Ray didn't need to know anything was going on between Alana and Locke. It wasn't any of Ray's business. And it was so early that whatever was developing, Alana barely knew what it might turn out to be. Maybe it wouldn't go anywhere, and maybe it would become something good. Something special. But who knew at this point?

She didn't want to mention it, just in case that almost kiss had been a heat-of-the-moment thing for Locke. It might not have even meant anything past that stairwell.

Locke watched Kaylee make a phone call while her sister and brother battled. Hand over her mouth, she spoke into the phone. No one heard, and he couldn't read her lips with her hand over them. Whatever she was up to, Kaylee was keeping it to herself.

His whole body ached from that fight with Daniel, but what Alana had said hurt more. He wasn't going to argue with it. He knew why, and Alana had simply caught him unawares. He was seriously not used to wearing his heart on his sleeve like this. His emotions didn't normally get this much airtime—especially not when he was supposed to be working.

"Locke."

He spun. William walked down the hall toward them, towing a still handcuffed Daniel Kaiko with him. Kaylee gasped. Alana went to her, then Ray. Kaylee held out Ray's phone and lifted her chin.

"Who did you—" Ray swiped the screen. "How is Mikio going to help with this?"

Kaylee glanced at Daniel. Locke didn't want to know what would happen if he got closer and Kaylee was forced to face the man who'd tied her to a chair and questioned her. He intercepted William before he brought the man too close to Kaylee. What was he thinking?

Locke frowned. "What is it?"

William said, "Sergeant Preston should be the one to take Daniel into custody, should he not?"

"If Daniel's done at the hospital. He was here to get treatment."

William nodded. "The doctor confirmed that has been completed. His wound has been stitched, and he needs to be taken to the police station." He glanced at Locke. "You can talk to him there. After you get your injuries seen to."

Daniel smirked.

Locke wasn't optimistic on his chances of being able to get the former SEAL to say anything he hadn't planned on saying anyway. He'd questioned suspects before, but not in a criminal investigation—only when an intruder attempted to break through White House security. The Secret Service wasn't a police force. Locke wasn't trained at breaking suspects and getting them to confess, but if Ray let him maybe they could question the man together.

"I'll go with Ray." He looked back at Alana, knowing the idea wasn't going to be a popular one with her brother, but maybe he could make peace with Ray, or try to. He might learn something about Alana in the process.

"Agent Preston, why don't you go, too?"

William's suggestion made Locke frown. "I guess we're all going, then." He looked at Ray. "Give us a minute?"

Ray took Daniel's arm and walked him away from where Locke stood with Alana and William. He looked at his colleague. "So everything is fine with the police and the president? I don't have to worry about the bomb threat?"

William nodded. "Yes, why wouldn't it be?"

Maybe because their phones were still fritzing, and Locke had been branded a traitor—at least in the eyes of the local police department. He blew out a breath, his injuries stinging. "Okay, then." He was going to check with Ray on that, as well. Find out why the man was so intent on assuming Locke was the bad guy here.

William motioned to Kaylee, who had her eyes closed again. "I'll get Ms. Preston settled back in her room and make sure that she's all right."

"Thank you." Alana glanced once at her sister, like she wanted to say something, and then walked toward her brother.

"I'll check in later, when we get back to the hotel." When William nodded, Locke went to join Alana and her brother, now walking Daniel to the elevator.

If William wanted to ask Kaylee about what was going on, then great. Maybe they'd get more answers with her opening up to someone she didn't know. Locke prayed the cops would find Brian Wells now that he'd stopped shooting. They needed to win on something here, considering it felt like they were just playing catch-up every second.

Daniel knew what was going on.

They climbed in the elevator, and Locke stared at the man. Finally Daniel turned, his gaze hard. Locke said, "Who hired you?"

Ray held Daniel's arm. He shook it once, hard and fast. Not the way Locke would have done it, but he understood Ray's frustration at both of his sisters being in danger because of this man and not being able to do anything about it. "The man asked you a question."

Daniel didn't respond to Locke.

"Sure, you could have planned it. You're not just a grunt, you're a SEAL."

"Not anymore."

"It's still there, though." Locke didn't figure the skills just melted away after a person was discharged, even dishonorably. That just meant Daniel was *angry* and trained. And Locke had the injuries to prove it. "You could have planned this, even with the mistake in targeting Alana—"

"Who says that was a mistake?"

Locke waved a hand toward her. "So you planned to swim up on her in the surf and…what, slit her throat?"

Daniel shrugged.

"Then you question Kaylee. Oh, after you killed Beatrice Colburn. Then Brian kills Zane Franks."

Daniel swallowed.

"Now he's gunning for Kaylee or Alana. Cleaning up your loose ends?" Locke stared him down. "Why would he need to do that if you'd done what you were supposed to do? I think you missed. You failed, more than once. Like you did in the navy."

"You don't know anything about it."

"You're right." Locke didn't know the reason Kaiko had been discharged, but it wasn't by doing what he should've done. "But I can guess." He paused. "Hot-headed? Probably had a problem with authority. Navy wasn't as lucrative as the yakuza, and the weather wasn't as good as it is in Hawaii. There's a lot of reasons the grass might be greener on the civilian side. But you didn't leave, they kicked you out."

Daniel's lips pressed together.

"Now you're mad. Your commander in chief didn't want your service anymore, so now…what? You're trying to put *him* out of service?"

Daniel said nothing.

"Is this a plot to kill the president?"

Silence.

"Does it have to do with the surf competition?" What had Kaylee discovered that led to her listing those four names she had the cop give to Alana? Locke sent a text to William to have him ask her and prayed it would go through.

"This will get put on you. All of it." Locke took a half step toward Daniel Kaiko. "If anything else happens. If the president is hurt. If anyone else is injured or killed, this all goes on your shoulders. I'll make sure you're charged with all of it while Brian Wells gets a couple counts of conspiracy."

"He killed that cop in the restaurant, not me."

So Daniel had heard that the man died in surgery. Locke hadn't even had the chance to tell Alana yet. "It won't matter whether it was Brian or not. You're part of this, and that cannot be denied."

The only way to get Daniel to turn on whoever had

hired him and Brian Wells was to play on his dislike of that person—his dislike of being forced into a corner. Daniel would need to reclaim the power, to fight back. Only with that would Locke have a real shot at getting the information out of him.

The elevator dinged.

Ray moved Daniel out of the car. Alana followed on their left and Locke took up position to their right.

Daniel glanced at Locke as they walked through the lobby. "You think I know who's behind this? What if all I have is text messages and instructions but no name?"

"Then I guess you'll have a long time in prison thinking about how you should've done things differently."

Locke had the phone, and they could trace those messages to their origin. But if that number was unregistered, it would be nothing but a dead end.

He held the door. Daniel came through with Ray and they fanned out again. As they hit the curb, Locke paused for a car to pass them before they could cross.

Daniel Kaiko's body jerked. Before Locke realized what happened, the man fell to the ground, taking Ray with him. There was a bullet-size hole in the former SEAL's forehead.

"Down!"

Alana, already crouching, dived for the ground and Locke did the same.

SIXTEEN

"I was wrong."

Alana glanced over. Ray was talking to Locke.

Daniel Kaiko lay dead between them. She turned away from the sight of it and stood, brushing off her clothes. No other shots had come. She hardly knew what to do. Maybe this was only the calm before another storm.

Alana scanned the rooftops, trying to see detail past the yellow glow of street lights. Skyscrapers neighbored this downtown hospital, and she looked over every window. Usually she enjoyed the heat of evening, but right now it felt too close. Too…something. She wiped the sweat from her face. Her stomach pinched with every move, and she laid her hand over the wound on her side.

Locke got up and strode over. "You okay?"

She should ask him the same. "I think I pulled it again when I landed. But you look worse than me."

"I'll be fine." He put his arm around her and pulled her close to his side. "I'm glad you're okay."

Alana hugged his middle, grateful they could take a moment to comfort each other without the added pressure of their feelings. Whatever happened on this trip, when they got home they would remain friends. She hoped. "He'd have shot us by now if he was going to, right?"

Locke nodded. "We should walk around, see if we can see him." He surveyed the buildings around them as she had done.

"I didn't see him."

"You can stay with Ray. I'll go."

Alana shook her head.

Ray said, "So both of you are just going to ignore the fact I'm standing here?"

Alana turned to her brother. "You have to stay with Daniel, right?" She didn't like his tone at all.

Ray nodded, but he didn't look happy. "Homicide will want to talk to you."

"We'll be back."

As Locke walked away, Alana followed. Ray called out, "I just wanted to say thank you. That was all."

She looked back over her shoulder at her brother. Ray almost looked like he felt guilty. Or sorry, at least. He told Locke, "You protected Alana. I just wanted to tell you I appreciated it."

Locke said, "It's my job. I'm just trying to do my best with it."

Alana winced, and thankfully Locke didn't see it. She didn't need him to throw those words back at her. Even if he was talking to Ray, he was only repeating what she'd said.

When they were out of earshot of her brother, Alana took out her ponytail and ran her hands through her hair, trying to inject some energy into her movements. When was the last time they ate? She wasn't the kind of person who could forsake food for long stretches of work and expect to operate at maximum capacity. Eventually she would fatigue. She retied her hair and looked around, watching the people and windows for Brian Wells.

"You okay?" He asked it, but he didn't look at her. Locke was on the job.

Did she want to admit to him that she needed to eat? It wasn't like she had a medical condition, just a normal person's need to consume food when she was expending so much energy. The day had been a roller coaster of adrenaline ups and downs and breakfast at the hotel had been a long time ago. She was starving. Probably a strange reaction to her life being in danger—again— but it was what it was.

Still, Locke looked more in need of medical attention than she was of food. He should get those cuts looked at. Locke said, "I know what it probably sounded like, me telling Ray exactly what you told him. I'm not taking it lightly, and I'm not brushing it off."

Alana said, "What?"

"Whatever's happening between us. You know...that kiss we nearly had." His eyes were warm, as though he'd been anticipating something good and even just the memory of it affected him. "It's just nothing to do with your brother."

"Oh."

"I figured a united front was the best option, so I told him exactly what you did."

Okay, so that wasn't a bad reason. She didn't like how it had sounded, but figured that just gave her a window into how it felt for him to hear her say that about them. It stung, basically. But his reasoning wasn't bad.

Alana looked at each person as they walked. Downtown was always busy, even this late in the day. "I just wasn't going to explain to my brother something that's none of his business. And why is he getting all big brothery on me now? Like it's his right to question you and make sure your intentions are good." She shook her head. "Where was he when—" Alana shut her mouth. There was no way Locke needed to hear about old teenage drama that had seemed like a big deal at the time.

"There's a story there."

"Sure." She smiled, making an older man passing in the other direction do a double take. "But there's no need for me to tell it to you."

Locke slowed and turned. They were stopped on the sidewalk, forcing people to part around them.

She looked up at him. "What?"

Locke didn't speak for a moment. Then he nodded, almost to himself, and said, "Six years ago there was this rookie. Her name was Tina."

Alana knew the story, but she wanted to hear it from Locke. "What happened?" Clearly it was something that had affected him deeply, or he wouldn't be looking at her so seriously.

"It was a routine trip. We were in Denmark, and the president was leaving a summit. Normal stuff. Everyone was jet-lagged and we just wanted to get back to the hotel. This was the last event of the day."

She took his hand and held it in hers. Locke gave her a small smile and continued, "Someone yelled, 'Gun.' Everyone thought a man in the crowd had pulled a gun and meant to kill the president. We moved with the president toward the car, but a delivery truck swerved. Tina was on the edge when it plowed toward the front doors of the conference center. She was hit by the truck. She died at the hospital. Doing her job. She was the one on that side of the formation, and there was nothing that could've changed it..." His voice faded out.

"But you still feel responsible."

"It was my team."

"It was a terrible accident."

Locke set his free hand on her shoulder. "It was a terrible accident, but it's also the job we do. And mine is to take care of the president *and* every team member."

"You aren't all powerful. If you were, I know you'd fix everything, but that's not the way it works. People are responsible for their own destiny. The agent. Tina. She was doing her job. What about the driver?"

"He was drunk, back on the job after his lunch break." Locke shook his head.

Alana moved closer to him. "It was a horrible thing, I don't doubt that. But we have to try to figure out how to move on from those things, maybe even how to use them to be better."

"Like your surfing accident."

Alana nodded. It had been hard, but she'd channeled all that drive to be the best into being a Secret Service agent, and in making her dad proud.

"How did you do it?"

"I found new dreams." She sighed. "Only now that I'm back here, it feels like everyone else didn't. Like they think I was wrong because I found something I want to do. It isn't resentment, but it feels similar. Blame, maybe."

She didn't want to think about surfing. Yes, she'd been really good, but it almost felt like they begrudged her for being a Secret Service agent now. As though she couldn't be successful at more than one thing, and she'd had her shot then lost it through injury.

Alana looked around just so she didn't have to look at Locke. The police hadn't found Brian Wells, either, and they were searching hard since one of their own had been shot in the restaurant. Was the man just so good of a sniper that he would be impossible to find?

"Alana." His hands were still on her shoulders.

She glanced at him then. "Yes?"

"I'm glad you're here. I'm glad you're okay. It's been close a couple of times, and you look like you're about to drop. You have to tell me when you need rest, or food. Because I want to be there for you, to help you."

Sure, that was nice. But still… "Locke, you can't blame yourself if anything happens to me. You can't control Brian Wells, just like you couldn't control Daniel Kaiko. Help is one thing, but you can't just protect me because you'd be torn up if I got hurt. That's like trying to control the situation by circumventing what might happen."

Locke pulled her to him then. He held her in his arms and pressed a kiss to her forehead. It was the sweetest kiss of her life. "Guess I have some things to learn, then. About trusting God. And about trusting you."

Alana leaned back. She touched his cheeks and pulled his face to hers so she could kiss his lips. It didn't last more than a second, but from the way her heart leaped in her chest, she wouldn't have guessed that. "We do this together. As partners."

He kissed her then. "Partners."

Locke wanted to hold her hand, but walking back to the hospital entrance he saw Ray spot them and decided against it. Sure, the cop had concluded Locke wasn't a bad guy. But while Ray might not be planning to arrest him, Locke figured he was on thin ice with Alana's brother. If they even had ice in Hawaii.

Ray called out, "No sniper?"

Locke shook his head. "We didn't spot him, but it was a long shot. He could be on any of these rooftops, in any window. He could be long gone or right under our noses."

Ray's expression morphed. Locke didn't like the facts, either, but Brian Wells had been trained to remain unseen. To go in, complete his assignment and get out, all without being discovered.

Ray said, "There are cops still out here, flashing his picture and looking for witnesses. Let's hope they find something."

Locke nodded. Beside him Alana remained quiet. He wanted to draw her out of her shell more. He'd shared something important with her, something painful. She didn't share his sense of guilt and had told him that he shouldn't blame himself, but it was how he felt. Tina was dead, and as her team leader the responsibility fell on him. Just as it would be on Locke's shoulders if anything happened to Alana now.

The rest of his team had been grafted into William's, tasked with protecting the president. He got updates, but they all knew the drill. Once the surf competition was ironed out, Locke and Alana would join them for the remainder of the trip. None of them argued when the fate of the president of the United States was in the balance.

Locke pulled out Daniel's phone and showed it to Ray. "Do you think—"

Alana darted away from them. Locke moved around Ray, just in case there was a threat. He didn't want her to face it alone. But it wasn't a threat. Kaylee Preston walked out of the hospital, leaning heavily on Mikio Adachi. She didn't look well; she was pale and clearly exhausted. Why was the woman leaving the hospital?

"Kaylee?" Alana approached her and Mikio. Locke glanced back. Sure enough, Mikio's car was parked at the curb, a yakuza soldier ready to open the door for them. They had a lot of courage to operate so brazenly in front of so many police officers and a crime-scene unit processing a murder scene. All the officers here knew who they were, but clearly Mikio didn't hide when he wasn't overtly doing anything wrong, which probably had the disadvantage of making Ray even more frustrated.

Kaylee met her gaze out of the corner of her eye. "Don't, Alana."

"Don't what?" His partner trailed behind Kaylee and Mikio as they made their way to his car, which was more of a limo than the vehicle he'd brought earlier. Evidently picking up his girlfriend warranted a more luxurious ride. "Kaylee, why are you leaving the hospital?"

"It isn't safe. I'm not going to stay here and be shot at."

"Can't we at least talk about this?"

They stopped by the car. Kaylee looked at Alana. For a few seconds she didn't say anything, then she nodded.

"Not out here. We're too exposed." Mikio glanced at Locke, and then said to Alana, "Get in."

Kaylee climbed in first. Alana next. Mikio went to get in, and Locke set his hand on the man's shoulder. The soldiers all tensed. Locke lifted his hands. "I want in on the conversation."

Mikio's lips thinned. "Very well."

Locke got in and moved to sit beside Alana on the

middle seats that faced the center. Kaylee sat at the back, and Mikio sat beside her. He put an arm around her, and she relaxed into his side.

Alana perched on the sideways seats, and Locke leaned back so he could see over her shoulder. He wouldn't get in the middle of their conversation, but if Alana was going to be in here, then it was where he would be, as well. Anything could happen, and if it did he would be with her.

"Kaylee, you think that Mikio can keep you safe?"

Alana wasn't pulling any punches, and he didn't want her to. Locke wanted to see her grow in strength, and part of that was her need to face down her sister. No matter what Kaylee threw at her, Alana needed to hold herself together. Otherwise she would never get past the default of reacting to Kaylee's emotions. She had to be able to…not disregard her sister's feelings, but operate in spite of them. It was the only way Alana could make peace with herself and what she'd made of her life.

Mikio shot Alana a look. "Of course I can keep your sister safe. Otherwise she wouldn't be leaving with me."

"Not that it's any business of yours," her sister said, "but I trust Mikio." Kaylee paused. "Are you really in this car to question his ability to keep me safe?"

Alana didn't rise to the bait. "I want to know about the four names on the list. You might be safe now, but the rest of us have a job to do. I need all the information I can get so that Locke and I can keep the president safe."

For a moment her sister looked proud, but the expression disappeared as fast as it had come. Locke wondered if Alana had even seen it.

"Okay, I'll tell you." Kaylee sighed. "It was at the

newspaper. I received an email that was sent to me by mistake—looked like a typo in the address. It was responding to an advertisement that had been posted on a social media account offering a couple of days' work at a local bookshop for cash. Beatrice answered that ad.

"I forwarded her email to the right person, but when I got a second email, about work at a gun shop, I looked into it more. The email said she'd seen the ad on her news feed so many times and she didn't normally do this kind of thing, but clearly they needed help because of the man she met at a coffee shop who mentioned it as well, so she was offering."

All of this was because an email was sent to the wrong person? Locke could hardly believe it. "We found an ad in Brian Wells's house, circled on the classifieds. Cash for two days' work at a gun shop. And we know a man visited him at the homeless shelter. Could be the same man, but who?"

Kaylee said, "Beatrice answered the email about the bookshop. But when I dug, I found out that the email address that the message should've reached had been closed—at least by the time I got to it. She might have received a reply after I let her know she sent it to me by mistake.

"So I went to see her. Beatrice locked up tight. Wouldn't tell me anything about the bookshop, not even its name or anything. And the email was generic, no mention of specifics. I never even knew whether she'd done the work. So I did more digging and found the same email address on two other ads, along with a phone number. From what I discovered, and what the guy in IT figured out, Daniel purchased a van from a buy/sell site online. Zane Franks told me he responded to an offer for a skydiving lesson."

Alana said, "You talked to him."

Kaylee nodded. "And now he's dead. Each of them answered something connected to the newspaper. Whoever brought them together did it using the newspaper, but there is no clear link between them other than that. And it's barely even a link, because every response was to something different."

"How did you know it was the four of them?" Alana asked. "Surely more people had to have responded."

"Only the four of them ever did. That's how I knew they were targeted, along with the fact someone spoke to Beatrice, and you said the same for Brian Wells. Maybe this man—whoever he was—visited all four of them. It was very specific, almost as though the ads had been designed to draw them in. I talked to this kid in our IT department who said online ads are targeted anyway. Searches, purchases—it's all tracked. I think the same was done with these ads. We know the man spoke to Beatrice and Brian. He must have been the extra nudge to get them to respond. Especially since Brian's was an insert in his paper."

Kaylee almost looked scared as she continued, "And it turns out the advertisements didn't even go to everyone. Whoever put them out used a virus on the advertisement to make sure only certain IP addresses were able to view the ad. The IT guy found it embedded in the email." She paused. "And the flyer Brian Wells received wasn't in the copies of the newspaper that everyone else got. At least that's as much as I could figure out from the research that I did and what the IT guy at the newspaper was able to put together."

"But they still might not have responded. There's no guarantee," Alana said. "Whoever it was couldn't be sure they'd actually take the offer."

Locke said, "So they'd have found someone else to take their place? Maybe there were others targeted, who were supposed to have been drawn in, and we'll never know who they are. Unless we find the computer they used."

Kaylee nodded. "The IT guy came up against a wall of some kind. He couldn't discover the origin of the virus. But they must have figured out we were digging, because the IT guy was in a car accident a week later. He's in a coma, and Daniel Kaiko came after me to find out what I know."

Alana glanced over her shoulder, and Locke shared her look. He couldn't believe it, either. She said, "It has to have been whoever is messing with our phones, as well."

"Agreed. We know we're looking for someone with a reasonable amount of technical expertise and knowledge of the Secret Service." But how did that help them find Brian Wells? "We need to give Daniel Kaiko's phone to the police department and have them look into it. Find out who was contacting him and if that has anything to do with this."

Alana nodded. She turned back to her sister, noting the smug look on Mikio's face. He knew exactly what was on the phone, but techs could get beyond the surface. Maybe they would find something he hadn't seen. Alana told her sister, "Be careful."

When it was clear Kaylee wasn't going to say anything back, Alana got out of the car.

Locke stayed one second longer. He pulled a business card from his wallet and held it out to Kaylee. "If you need anything, I want you to call me."

It was Mikio who took the card.

SEVENTEEN

Alana had tried to hide her sadness after she got out of their car, but Locke could tell it affected her that her sister was in danger. Kaylee had decided to rely on someone who wasn't family, and Locke doubted that either Kaylee or Mikio was going to call him. But he could hope.

He'd wanted to say something, but Alana had walked straight up to Ray on the street outside the hospital and asked him to get what information he could from Daniel's phone. So they'd followed him to the police station, where Ray had dropped them off with the technician and then disappeared to his desk.

"Whoever messed with this phone knows what they're doing. But not everything has been deleted." The technician tapped keys on his keyboard. He'd plugged the phone in and was now attempting to access it.

"There are a couple of conversations in here, but it's clear from the messages that we're not getting everything. Mikio deleted whole threads, the call history—and all the photos. But what he did leave us with is telling. Plans to meet. Talk about a job, coming from a private number. It'll take time, but I might be able to get you the number."

Locke nodded. "Whatever you can give us will be great." He set a hand on Alana's back and rubbed up and down. Ray was gone, but that wasn't the only reason Locke decided to touch her now. She looked like she badly needed a friend, and when she smiled at him he knew he'd done the right thing.

"If you want the call history, you'll need a warrant for the service provider. Though there's no guarantee they'll give you the information—whether the phone is registered or not."

"At least we know he was communicating with someone. Daniel was receiving instructions, maybe. Which means if it's not Brian Wells, then someone else is telling them what to do."

Alana nodded. "The question that needs answering is who it is."

The technician said, "Let me keep looking. I'll try to find out if there are any voice mails stored online. And I'll go through his apps. A couple of his social media accounts are still logged on."

"Thank you," Locke said. "Even if you don't come up with anything, we appreciate you doing this for us."

Alana glanced at him again. Was she surprised that he was able to be polite? Or maybe just surprised that he would do it at a time like this?

Ray returned with coffee. It tasted awful, but it would keep them awake for the rest of the night. The surf competition was tomorrow, and they didn't even know if they would be able to join the rest of the agents in protecting the president as he attended. Locke was ready to get back to his regular duties, but first they had to figure this out.

"Did the police turn up anything in the hunt for Brian Wells?"

Ray shook his head. "We'll be the first to know if they do. They're still searching the streets, and I'm eager to talk to him about the fact that he shot up my sister's hospital room."

Locke figured Alana felt the same way. They hung out while the technician muttered and typed and then muttered some more. Eventually he said, "Bingo."

"What is it?" Ray asked, crowding closer to see the screen. "What did you find?"

Locke glanced at the screen, but it looked like a downloaded file and not text that he could read. The technician clicked it, and what loaded looked like a map.

Alana gasped. "That is the layout for the surf competition tomorrow. It's where all the vendors are going to set up so they know what spot belongs to them and what spots belong to the food trucks and the merchandise tables."

"So what is Daniel Kaiko doing with a copy of this?" Ray asked.

The technician said, "It was sent to him by an anonymous social media account that's been deactivated now. He received it a few days ago, through the messaging app, but there weren't any instructions. I can see if I can trace its origin but that will take time."

"So we have no idea why he needed this," Locke said. "But whatever it is, it was serious enough that when we got Daniel into custody he was killed by Brian Wells before he could tell us anything. Something is going down, and it's probably happening at the surf competition."

"We have to find out if the person who sent this to him knew the president would be there," Alana said.

"It could be a plot to assassinate POTUS. Brian Wells is the only one left that we know of, but he is fully capable of executing a hit on the president all by himself and doesn't have help."

Locke ran his hands down his face. He'd encountered danger many times over, but he'd never been part of an active investigation into a plot to kill the president. Even in the Secret Service it wasn't an everyday occurrence. An active shooter had easier targets than their commander in chief, but someone wanted to make a splash. It was up to Locke and Alana to figure out who it was and then stop them.

First course of action for Locke was to call it in and warn the president and the teams that they had reason to believe someone would try to kill the president tomorrow.

"We need to send that to William. He has to know that security has been compromised. Once he has that, we can move forward." Locke turned to the technician. He handed over his cell phone. "Can you look at this now and tell me why it's acting weird? Alana's, too. We think somebody is hindering our ability to connect with our people."

The technician nodded. "I can do that." While the technician tinkered with both of their phones, the three of them moved away.

Ray glanced between Locke and Alana. "I want to be part of the security for tomorrow. Law enforcement needs to be on the ground, even more than normal. They'll be there for the competition anyway, and more so because the president is there. But if we know for sure that someone is targeting him, we have to be prepared. There's no way I'm gonna let the president get assassinated in my jurisdiction."

Locke figured if he was a police officer he would feel the exact same way. "I'll get you William's number. You can coordinate between your captain and him."

Alana perched on the edge of the table. "There's a lot we have to do before tomorrow if we're going to make sure this goes off without a hitch. But the best thing would be if we could convince the president to stay in his hotel."

"And not see his niece compete?" Locke didn't agree, but he knew how stubborn the president was even when there was a threat.

There was always a threat.

Alana didn't think it was an awful idea to try to convince the president to stay at the hotel tomorrow. Sure, he didn't get the chance to see his niece compete all the time, but he had to understand the circumstances. She knew for a fact that he understood he faced these types of situations. She was certain that if she and Locke could speak with him, they could convince him it was in his best interest to stay away.

"I want to at least try."

Locke studied her face and finally nodded. "It is a good idea. But we have to be prepared to deal with it if he decides he's still going to attend."

Ray sipped his coffee. "Isn't that just like high-class babysitting? I don't know if I could do that job. But I guess there are parts of my job you guys wouldn't enjoy. You know, like procedure, and letting other people do their jobs while you're trying to do yours."

"We don't need your attitude, Ray," Locke said. "That's not what we're talking about. And it's not helpful to either of us for you to keep throwing out back-handed comments."

Alana said, "We need your help, Ray. That's why we're here. Because you offered to help us, and not because it's so nice for you to talk like that to us."

She glanced at Locke in time to see him swell with pride, even though she was being sarcastic. It had been cathartic to face down her siblings the way she had today. To see her sister and not have to take on board Kaylee's emotions. To be the recipient of her brother's attitude and not have to respond to it. Or rise to it. She could do what she wanted, and she knew Locke was going to stand by her no matter what. Because they were partners.

"If you have something to say that will help us," Locke said, "that's fine. But our job is a very specific one. We don't need you putting us down for doing what we're trained to do."

Alana wanted Ray to see that she had risen above their opinions and done something amazing with her life. She was serving a purpose. Couldn't her family appreciate that?

Ray lifted both hands, palms out. "Okay, okay. I get the fact you guys are on the same team. One that I'm not a part of. Excuse me if that rubbed me the wrong way."

"We're not trying to rub you the wrong way," Alana said. "We're just trying to explain to you that you're making this harder for us and not easier."

"I'm sorry, okay." Ray had the decency to look like he felt bad. "Maybe I might actually be a tiny bit jealous. Maybe I wanted to do something amazing and I have to watch *you* do it instead. Again."

Alana's eyes widened. "I thought you were mad at me for leaving. You told me not to be a cop."

"I wasn't mad, but you left me with Kaylee, and I have no idea how to understand that girl. She never quits asking questions and gets herself into trouble all the time. I'm constantly shoveling her out of problems she's gotten herself into. Then she goes and falls in love with Mikio Adachi, of all people, and I'm supposed to be okay with that? Dad would never have let her do this, but I can't tell her no, because I'm just her brother and what do I know?"

Alana stepped closer. "You could have asked me for help. Kaylee wanted me to go—"

"You keep saying that," Ray interrupted. "But I just don't think it's true."

"She yelled at me to get out. She told me I wasn't welcome in her life." Alana paused. "But you could have called me and asked for help. You never did, so I didn't know there was anything wrong."

Ray opened his mouth, but his phone rang. He answered it, his eyes still on Alana. "Yes, thank you. Okay, we'll be right there." He motioned to the technician. "Grab your cell phones, or leave them here. But my officers found Brian Wells."

Locke said, "We'll leave them if there's a chance we can find out who's messing with them."

Within twenty minutes they were on a downtown street not far from the hospital. Police had the area surrounded and traffic blocked off. They'd parked behind Ray, a couple streets over. Now Locke followed the sergeant through the police barrier, and Alana stayed right behind them. "Are they holding him somewhere?"

Ray glanced over his shoulder as they strode toward a man wearing a police captain's uniform. "Let's find out what's happening."

She figured that was kind of an answer to her question. The police captain motioned them over with a wave of his hand. When they were close enough to hear, he said, "We have Brian Wells cornered just up there." He pointed at a restaurant. The alley right beside it ran between the two buildings.

"Let's go," Locke said. "We wouldn't want to keep the man waiting."

Alana nodded. The three of them drew their weapons and approached the alley. The man crouched at the end had a suitcase about the size of a violin case on the ground beside him. It could easily have been a bomb, but she figured it was more likely his rifle.

The only problem was that this was not Brian Wells.

"It's not him," Alana said to Ray, while keeping her attention on the man. "This isn't Brian Wells. Although someone did a good job, because it looks like him." She even thought that she might've seen this man earlier, at the soup kitchen. He had the same air about him that Brian Wells possessed.

"Well, who is he, then?"

Locke said, "I guess we probably could just ask him." He turned to the man. "Is that your suitcase?"

The man shook his head, extremely nervous. He had no visible weapons but could still be dangerous. They were going to have to tread carefully.

The man said, "He paid me to take it, and the hat and his jacket. Told me to walk around. I figured for five hundred bucks I wasn't going to complain about staying downtown when I could be on the beach."

Was there any point in asking where Brian Wells might have gone? Alana figured the man was in the wind. Long gone.

Locke said, "Kick the case over to me. Do it nice and slow, and I'll get all this cleared up with the police."

The man did as Locke had asked, then said, "I didn't know who he was. I figured just another street bum, but he isn't, is he? He did something bad and now I'm caught up in it. All because I needed money." He shook his head.

Ray kept his gun aimed at the man, probably just as a precaution. Locke knelt and unclipped the case. Alana looked over and saw that inside it the foam had been spaced out, leaving a hole the size and shape of a sniper rifle.

Locke stood up.

Ray sighed. "I guess we're done here, then."

"So it's back to square one?" Alana blew out a breath. This had been a real shot at securing the safety of the president, but it was nothing.

Locke nodded. "Time to go and convince the president to stay at the hotel tomorrow."

Ray nodded. "I'll stay here."

Alana didn't want to talk to her brother much longer anyway, so that was fine with her. He could stay here and do his job while they left to do theirs. She saw Locke glance at her as they walked back to the car. She said, "Don't ask me if I'm okay."

At least he had the decency to smile. Alana shook her head. "Sorry, I guess all this has me on edge."

"After we talk to the president, we'll know more. And we'll be able to rest. Get some food and some sleep."

"That sounds great." Alana walked beside him to the gathered crowd behind the police barrier. "Why do I feel underdressed without my phone?"

Locke didn't think it was funny, though. Alana tugged on his arm and then trotted back to her brother. "Ray, can I use your phone?"

When he handed it over, she called the technician and asked if he had an update.

"Not on Daniel's phone, but there's something interesting on both of yours. And that iPad."

Alana put the phone on speaker so Locke could hear, and then said, "What is it?"

"A worm. These three devices have all been infected. You downloaded an app that mimics a loss of signal, among other things. I've seen it before. Your devices are working fine, except that this app masks that and alters what it wants. Everything sent and received goes through it, so they can filter what they want and doctor anything."

Alana blew out a breath. This was crazy.

"Then the app takes it a step further," the technician said. "It disrupts everything. You can't use these devices at all unless you wipe them. Full factory reset. But that's not the bad part."

Locke frowned at Alana and asked the technician, "What is it?"

"From what I have it looks like the blueprints on Daniel's phone came from your phone, Locke."

Alana gasped. It was Locke who said, "Thank you."

Alana hung up and gave the phone back to her brother. Locke tugged her to the car. When she looked at him to find out if he was even taken aback like she was, he said, "I know."

But he evidently set it aside and drove to the hotel so they could meet up with their team. Three miles later he glanced into the rearview mirror and stared for longer than usual.

"What is it?"

"I'd say maybe nothing. If it was any other day than today."

He was just done speaking when the van behind them clipped the back of their vehicle. Someone in the passenger seat threw an object from the window. Alana had just figured out what it was when the grenade exploded in front of them, bathing the hood of the car in flames.

EIGHTEEN

Alana screamed. Locke gripped the steering wheel and fought the urge to hit the brakes. Nothing would be served by them careening into a building on the side of the road. This was a busy area, and people were running for their lives. Screaming. Pretty soon cops would be on their tail, but until then he had to hang on.

Whoever was behind them, it wasn't only one person. So if Brian Wells was in the van, he had a partner. One who was currently throwing grenades at them.

Locke wanted to tell Alana everything was going to be fine, but he couldn't when he didn't know that for sure. All he could do was pray, and he was.

The van was behind them still. Locke wove through traffic, and they kept pace with him through every intersection and every turn. Whoever they were, the driver had skill. But from what Locke could see, neither of them was an old man—both had dark hair. They almost looked like yakuza, but that could mean the man protecting Alana's sister had sent some of his men to kill them. And that meant the man was involved in this plot.

And they hadn't seen his deception.

"What can we do?" Alana glanced around. "What if

we just pull over? We have skill. We're trained, and we have guns. They want to kill us, but we're not going to go down without a fight."

Locke wasn't so hot on the idea of getting into a gunfight in the middle of a busy street. Still, the idea was a better one than keeping moving. If they stopped, the police would arrive faster, but there could also be casualties. Then again, there could be casualties if they kept going. *Lord, what do we do? How do we end this and keep everyone safe?* "We need the cops to hurry up."

The van pursued them for another two blocks before the passenger emerged from the sunroof. Asian. Was he yakuza? The man lifted a machine gun out of the van and perched it on the swerving vehicle as they turned a sharp corner. When both vehicles straightened, he opened fire.

The back window of their vehicle was the first to go as it shattered into millions of pieces. Locke pushed Alana's head between her knees, trying to get her out of the line of fire.

Even if they still had their phones, he didn't know if they would have even been able to call someone. Plenty of people on the street had cell phones, and emergency dispatch was probably receiving an influx of calls at this very moment. Locke would have preferred to call them himself, but the last time he'd done that he was accused of trying to plant a bomb to kill the president. It probably was better that other people were coming to their aid now.

"I hear sirens," Alana said from her lap. "The cops will probably set up some kind of barrier and force us and them to stop."

Locke agreed. He was ready for whatever they were

going to do. He just wanted Alana out of the line of fire. If the two men behind them weren't killed—which if this was done right they would not be—he could find out why they were doing this.

Up ahead the cops had arranged themselves so that three vehicles blocked the two-lane road. Across the street they had laid out a spike strip. "Lift your head, Alana. This is going to be a bumpy end."

He wasn't used to having this much help, and it hadn't exactly aided them so far, but he was willing to take the assistance now.

The occupants of the van tried one more round of attack. The passenger threw another grenade, which hit a police car and exploded the windows. Locke glanced away from the brightness of the flames just as more gunshots came from the van, but there was nowhere for the van to go. As it pulled up beside them, Locke looked for a road they could pull onto at the last minute. But there wasn't one. The police had set up in the perfect spot. Locke and Alana would hit the strip and their vehicle would be disabled, but the same thing would happen to the van.

Seconds later they hit it. Locke fought the wheel as the vehicle juddered and tried to swerve on its own. The van clipped their bumper. Police officers dived for cover, their guns drawn. Locke directed their car out of the way as best he could, but cops were everywhere. He hit the front end of a black-and-white at full speed and grunted at the impact. The air bags deployed. Alana cried out, but it cut off sharply. He hit the brakes, and when they were slow enough he pulled up the parking brake as well and then put the car in Park.

Locke threw his door open and almost fell out of the

car, his leg smarting where Daniel had cut him. The cops had the van surrounded. It lay on its side close to where he had stopped. He drew his weapon as well, and assisted with cover as the cops pulled two men from the van. It hadn't been smart to do this. They had to have known the police would stop them. Locke needed to question them to be sure, but their orders must not have been to hurt Locke and Alana. This wasn't more than a diversion. Something to take the police's attention from elsewhere, to delay Locke and Alana from getting back to the hotel to speak with the president.

But would Mikio really go to these lengths just to obstruct Locke and Alana's plans?

When they had the two men in the back of a black-and-white, Locke went back over to the SUV. Alana hadn't gotten out of her side. He opened the door, and Alana slumped to the side, into his arms. Blood ran from her nose, but it didn't look bad enough to be broken.

"Alana, can you hear me?" Locke wanted to make her wake up, but it was probably a good thing she wasn't conscious to feel her injuries. A lot had happened to her the past few days. Not much of it had been peaceful or good, but she had been a trouper through all of it.

She moaned but didn't open her eyes. Locke gathered her closer to him and put his chin on her head. If someone had wanted to distract them, they'd succeeded. They had hit Locke in the place where it hurt the most and forced him to turn his attention from the president's safety to taking care of his partner. Because he was going to make sure Alana was safe.

Somewhere along the way, she had become more important to him than his job, and Locke was never going to apologize for that. Whoever was behind this—

whether or not it was Mikio—knew him. Maybe they even knew his history and that he blamed himself for Tina's death.

As he looked down at his unconscious partner, Locke realized that if he was going to save the president, he had to set aside his feelings for Alana. If it could be used against him, then it was a liability. And liabilities cost his job. If the president was killed because Locke was distracted by Alana, all of them would lose.

He had to let her go.

From the moment Alana had woken up in the front seat of the police car she'd somehow been transferred into while unconscious, until now standing beside Locke watching the interrogation, things had been weird. The two men who had shot at them on the road had been separated and were being questioned by the police. Locke and Alana had picked up their phones and the iPad from the technician, and now the interview they were watching was being conducted by Ray, who was questioning the driver of the van.

But Alana's attention was not on what was happening on the other side of the window. It was on the man beside her. She didn't understand what had happened to Locke while she'd been knocked out. He was so different, barely looking at her. Hardly talking to her and certainly not touching her. Maybe he would prefer it if she wasn't even here, if she was out of his way, maybe even at the hospital. But she wasn't interested in seeing a doctor for her aches and pains if he wasn't going to do the same. Alana wanted to know why those two men had tried to kill them.

Through the window, Ray sat at the table with his

back to them. "Nice tattoo. I feel like I've seen something like that before. Any chance you know Mikio Adachi?"

The man facing Ray didn't move in his chair. His expression didn't change. His straight black hair was slicked to the side. "I have no idea who that is."

"Sure you don't," Ray said. "But I'm guessing you know Daniel Kaiko, right? His number is right here in your phone. Seems like he called you yesterday. Want to tell me what the two of you talked about?"

The man sniffed and flicked his hair back. "I told him we were out of milk." His mouth curled up in a sneer. "Told him to pick some up on his way to the dinner party his sister was having."

Ray leaned back in his chair. "So if we bring his sister in here, she'll corroborate what you're saying? She might be able to provide you with an alibi for last night, but I want to know why you chased two Secret Service agents in a van and tried to kill them."

Alana swelled with pride watching her brother work. He was as good a cop as their dad had been, and Ray had succeeded in following in his footsteps. She felt the small smile play on her lips as she watched him, completely relaxed, working the conversation around in his favor.

Daniel had been eliminated, but someone out there was still active. The question was whether Brian Wells was working alone now, or not.

"Who says I was trying to kill those agents?" the man asked. "Maybe I was just driving down the street and they shot at me first. Yeah, that's right. It was self-defense."

Ray lifted his hands for a second. "Am I seriously supposed to believe that two Secret Service agents decided to shoot you just for fun? I think you know what happened to Daniel on the street outside the hospital earlier today. I think you know what he was involved in, and all about Brian Wells. But why try to kill two Secret Service agents if they weren't the ones responsible for Daniel's death?"

"You think I'm avenging him? Daniel had his own stuff going on." The man looked around, not meeting Ray's eyes. He was obviously hiding something, but whether or not it had anything to do with what he'd done remained to be seen. If he was a yakuza soldier, then he was likely involved in a number of things he wouldn't want to tell Ray about. But that was fine with Alana—Ray could deal with that stuff on his own. All they needed to know right now was what this man knew about Daniel's activities.

Ray said, "How did Daniel get along with Mikio?" When the man said nothing, Ray continued, "How about his choice of woman?"

The man's eyebrows rose. "You think I'm so dumb I don't know Kaylee Preston is your sister?"

Ray said, "Ah, so you do know Mikio."

"Whatever, yeah, Daniel didn't like that much. He's a traditionalist, doesn't think the head of the yakuza should be with a woman who isn't Japanese."

Alana figured it was plausible that was the main reason Daniel didn't like Kaylee. But it likely wasn't the only reason.

"Did you share his sentiments?"

He shrugged at Ray's question.

"He's dead now. What does it matter if you agreed with him or not? Life goes on, am I right?"

The man's eyes hardened. "You don't know anything about me."

Ray flipped open the paper file. "Two counts of assault, one of theft."

"That was years ago, and I did my time."

"You're out on parole. What do you think is going to happen when I tell your parole officer you were chasing two Secret Service agents, throwing grenades and firing at innocent people in the street trying to murder a couple of feds?"

"That was Tai! Not me!" He slammed both fists onto the table. "I never fired a shot, and the grenades weren't my idea."

"Why was Tai trying to kill them?"

"For Daniel. They just stood there and did nothing. And yeah, I was mad, but I didn't agree we should kill them. I thought he was just going to scare them a little."

Ray shifted in his seat. "I could charge you with reckless endangerment and a bunch of other things. You'll be back in prison before you can blink." He paused. "Unless…"

"Get on with it." The man's face twisted into a grimace. "Make your deal and then *leave me alone*."

"He'll take it," Locke muttered. "Doesn't matter much what Ray offers him."

Alana's attention was pulled from the window. When she looked at Locke, it didn't make her feel better. His eyes were still guarded. Where was the man who'd kissed her so sweetly earlier? She opened her mouth to ask what was wrong with him, but he turned away.

Dismissed her.

Alana swallowed. Inside the interrogation room, the driver said, "Daniel told us all about the job. He didn't want anyone else to know." He shrugged. "Maybe he thought he'd just disappear one day and we wouldn't know what happened to him, so he told us about the texts. About Brian Wells. Now Wells killed him, and those two Secret Service agents just stood there. With you. And *did nothing*." His face twisted again. "Maybe Tai was right and they did need to die. Wells didn't finish the job, but I coulda."

Ray didn't move. Alana curled her hands into fists. She didn't want to react to this man's threat, or think about someone else coming after her. But her stomach still hurt, and her nose and eyes were all swollen. She needed a vacation from Hawaii. She wanted Locke to hug her instead of barely looking at her. What had happened to them that was making him act like this?

Ray asked, "What would you have done after that? Daniel is dead. If he told you what he was supposed to do…"

The man grinned then. More scary than humorous. Alana took an involuntary step back. He said, "No point in trying to stop it. Daniel's part is done."

"Are you telling me you're part of a plot to assassinate the president?"

His eyes widened. "The pres…" His voice sputtered.

"That's what Daniel was doing," Ray said. "As far as we can tell, he was employed to be part of a team that's planning to kill the president. Now only Brian Wells is left." He paused. "Or so we thought."

"It's too late." Now he was panicked. "The package has already been delivered."

"To the surf competition?"

He nodded. "It's too late."

Ray tossed his pen on the table. "Tell me everything."

NINETEEN

"So the president doesn't believe us?" Alana stood outside the entrance to the surf competition, one hour until the start. The president wasn't due to be there until his niece's first heat. A reprieve, but only a short one.

"It isn't that he didn't believe us, it's that William objected so strongly and he had to make a decision." Locke didn't look happy at all. In fact, she didn't think she'd ever seen him this frustrated. "Since there's no consensus between us, the president decided that if we can't agree, he's going to play it carefully but he's still going to come."

Alana let her eyebrows rise.

"I know." Locke nodded. "William disregarded it all so fast I didn't even get a chance to tell the president half of what's happened the last few days." He blew out a breath. "If we were in Washington, I would try to convince him to use a body double. But there's no one here who can be briefed in time. Everyone would see through it."

"I've been thinking about who might be behind this." Alana hardly wanted to say it out loud. She couldn't even believe she was thinking about this. It was crazy, wasn't it?

"Whatever you're thinking, you need to tell me." He stepped closer to her and held both of her elbows. "I trust your judgment, Alana. And you can trust me, whether or not you think this idea is dumb."

She smiled at that. "It's just that this person seems to always be one step ahead of us. Ever since Daniel caught me off guard in the ocean, whoever hired him and Brian seems to be the one on top of things. All we've done is react, trying to figure out the plot." She paused for a moment before she said it, making sure that her coms were off. Locke could still use his, but she didn't want her words being transmitted over the Secret Service's radio frequency. "What if it's one of us? What if the person who hired Brian and Daniel is a Secret Service agent?"

People wandered past them. Locke scanned the crowd, as she did. But neither of them had been tasked with wanding people. There were plenty of security measures they could employ, but nearly every one of them depended on each of their team members doing a superior job and no one complaining about how long it took. No one wanted to be the example of how terribly human error could turn out.

That was why they trained over and over again and became as familiar as possible with the methods they had in place to protect the president. So that they weren't the weak link that cost the president his life.

Locke studied her face. "I think it's entirely possible that the person behind this could be a Secret Service agent. But that's because I always add it to the threat list."

Her heart sank. He didn't believe her.

He said, "I'm not saying you aren't right, but it's unlikely that one of us set this up. Think about it—if one of us was behind this, they wouldn't have chosen the surf competition. They would have chosen a different part of this vacation. There are easier-to-control spaces. There are easier-to-manage opportunities where you could secure success in a way that you never could on this beach with all of these people. Because we know where the kinks in our coverage are."

Alana nodded. "I see your point, and I know it sounds crazy, but it's the only thing that makes sense to me. How else would they know how to get into our tech and mess with your reports?"

She hadn't slept hardly at all the night before. Alana could only think that her sister was in danger, she was in danger herself and now the president was in danger. Locke was able to handle so much, but could he handle this, as well? She wanted to believe in him, and the God he trusted. Could she trust Him, too?

Alana wanted to go back to that belief of her childhood, to the faith she'd held on to so tightly before her surfing accident. But she didn't know how to approach Him when she'd walked away and left so many things unresolved. To return now would be to dig every one of those things out from where she had buried them. It meant making peace with Him the way she was trying to do with her sister, and that endeavor was turning out to be slow and painful.

She wanted to trust that He would accept her with no judgment, but she just wasn't at the point she could believe it. Not yet, at least.

Locke said, "We should keep our eyes open for anything that doesn't feel right."

"What if it's the man who met with Beatrice, and

Brian?" She wasn't sure she liked this idea anymore. She didn't want to be right. Almost as much as she didn't want to be wrong.

"If it means the difference between the president being alive or dead at the end of the day, then yes. That's exactly what I mean."

Alana blew out a breath and looked around. A couple of girls in their early twenties were watching her. She had figured that at some point someone here was going to recognize her. Not so much with the teen crowd, but those in their early twenties probably grew up hearing stories of her surfing and attended events like this to see her compete. She'd won a lot of trophies and become pretty well-known through her sponsor—at least in Hawaii and on the coast of California—before she got hurt. Even her injury had been widely publicized, and her social media account and email at the time had exploded with messages and comments of commiseration for what had happened to her.

Alana's life had been every surfer's horror story, the one thing they never wanted to happen to them. Some had even been glad it was her, and told her as much.

These girls might know who she was, but whether or not they were going to be friendly about it was anyone's guess. She just hoped they weren't going to get in the way if things got crazy.

"Don't look so worried," Locke said. "We've done everything we can. We checked all deliveries that had come in so far and then made sure only what we deemed safe was allowed to be brought in today. Foot traffic is a separate issue, but our teams know no one is allowed in with a backpack that hasn't been checked thoroughly by them."

She nodded. "It was a good idea to tell them to check for yakuza tattoos, as well. And you're right, we have done everything we can. Now all we need to do is keep our eyes and ears open. If Brian Wells shows up, we'll know about it."

She looked over at the ocean. There were a few surfers preparing for their heats, getting warmed up. A few just having fun in some good waves. If she didn't have a wound on her side she would have figured out a way to get in there with them. Alana would have argued she was checking for someone like Daniel who might sneak up and possibly hurt somebody—maybe even the president's niece.

She took a couple of steps closer to the edge of the water. They might even have a boat anchored off shore, as some did to take photos of the surf competition from the other direction. Crowd shots, and such, especially with the president rumored to be attending.

"What is it?" Locke stepped up behind her. "What are you thinking?"

She loved that he trusted her instincts in this, a world she knew so well. "A yacht. Brian Wells could set up out there and take whatever sniper shot he wanted. We would never be able to catch him in time. He could speed away and find an inlet to hide in."

From a boat there were plenty of places to go ashore and get lost in the dense jungle. Alana chewed on her lip and thought it through. "We need to have the police check every boat, just in case Brian Wells is hiding in one with his rifle waiting for the president to arrive."

Locke squeezed her bicep. "Good idea. I'll get in touch with the police chief and get that done."

Alana nodded but didn't look at him as he walked

away. He might be willing to trust what she knew of the surfing world to help him in his job as director, but they had lost something in all this. The friendship they had built so fast had disappeared just as quickly, and she didn't know if they would ever be able to get it back.

Locke was here with her, supporting her, but only as her team leader. She figured his ease with her just now had been almost involuntary, despite his obvious decision to pull away. He was fighting the pull that was between them, but he needed to get over it. Either they had all of this between them, or nothing at all.

Alana wasn't going to settle for halfway.

Locke found a police lieutenant and told him their suspicions. Alana had been right about a lot of things, and he was willing to trust her. She was as invested in this as he was, and it felt good to work together. He wanted to keep her safe but just couldn't allow himself to get involved any more than that. What if she died like Tina had? What if one of them didn't make it through this, and the other one was forced to live the rest of their life alone?

Locke didn't want to be the one who had to suffer, but neither did he want that for Alana. It had been hard enough after Tina died, knowing he was culpable in her death. Yes, it was selfish to shut himself off from Alana now—and he knew that she saw it even as he was doing it—but he was protecting both of them and not just himself.

If she was right and there really was someone within the Secret Service who was working against them, then there was no time to relax. No time to get distracted. They had to be fully focused on what was going on around them. Only if everyone on both teams worked together could they make sure that the president was safe from Brian Wells and whoever was behind the plot. Nothing suspicious had gotten into the surf competition in a truck, and everything here had already been checked. They had even brought bomb dogs from the local police station to walk through the area, and none of them had signaled an explosive device.

Maybe they were wrong and there was nothing here. It was possible, but they just couldn't take that risk with the president's life.

Locke still couldn't believe that William hadn't agreed with him. The other director had claimed he couldn't see the connection in all this that Locke could see. Even after Locke had relayed the intel Ray had gleaned from the man driving the van, William still didn't see a connection between attacks on Alana and her sister and a threat to the president's life. He'd cited the fact Daniel Kaiko hadn't been on any watch list. And the suspect Ray had interviewed hadn't even known that Daniel's intention had been to hurt the president.

In the end the president had decreed that they would play it safe but that he would still attend the surf competition.

That was why Locke intended to figure this out before the man even got here.

He walked back over to where Alana stood chatting with a couple of girls. Everyone except the Secret Service was in a bathing suit or shorts and a T-shirt. He felt as out of place in his suit as all of the other agents likely did.

Later they could get comfortable. Right now was about work.

Alana smiled as he approached. One of the girls checked him out, very obviously, and he would've blushed at any other time but right now all he could see was Alana, not looking the slightest bit uncomfortable in her skirt and blouse. At least one of them was at home here.

"Is this your boyfriend?" one of the girls asked. They both giggled.

Locke wanted her to say yes, but she didn't. And why would she have? He'd basically shut her off since they were shot at by the two men in the van.

Alana said, "He's actually my boss."

"Does that mean he's available?"

"It means he's working." Alana shooed both of them away and rolled her eyes. She didn't look happy that the girls had asked about his relationship status.

"Thanks for doing that," he said as a way of making peace. "I don't know how to break it to them gently when that happens. I usually come off looking like a giant jerk." He glanced from the two retreating girls back to Alana. Then he saw her face.

"Yeah, I noticed." She started to walk away.

"Alana, wait up."

She shook her head but didn't slow down. "I don't want to talk about this, Locke. Not right now, and not when you seem to change your mind on a dime. One minute everything's fine, and the next minute you won't even look at me. Now we're back to friends all of a sudden." She lifted her hands and let them fall back to her sides.

Locke stopped and let his shoes sink into the sand. He wanted to go after her, but she was right that he had changed his mind. Yes, from her point of view it was sudden, and she would be right, but they had to get to work right now. This is not the time to be distracted by regret and the feelings he shouldn't have for a colleague.

He caught up with her again but didn't say anything, just walked beside her as they scanned every booth, every entrance and exit. Every person. The Secret Service was at work, and together they could make things as safe as possible for the president and all the people who were here. The last thing they needed was mass casualties.

Alana was stopped two more times by people who recognized her. And while she made it clear she was busy she handled it with grace, keeping the conversations short and politely declining invitations to sign their gear. He was proud of her and scanned the area while she stood talking with them.

At the end of the two rows of tents selling merchandise, Locke saw a man walking from left to right across the center; he then disappeared behind a tent facing the beach. It was only a glimpse, but even wearing a baseball cap the man resembled Brian Wells. He looked back at Alana, but she was deep in conversation. It would only take a moment to check whether it was the right man.

Locke radioed the rest of the team to let them know he had a possible sighting of Brian Wells and then jogged toward where he'd seen the man go. He wove between people doing their shopping, saying, "Excuse me," a couple of times. He got to the tent at the end of the row, drew his gun and turned the corner. He was not willing to take any chances in this. Not when people he cared about were at risk.

The man who might have been Brian Wells was nowhere. Locke turned and scanned all directions, looking for the man he had seen. Nothing. Only one tent, set back from all the others, was a possibility for where he might have gone, though it was too obvious to be more than just a simple hiding place. Locke approached slowly, looking around for backup. But no one had come.

He entered the tent. It took a second for his eyes to adjust from the bright sun of outside to the relative darkness inside.

Movement behind him brought his attention around, but it was too late. Solid metal slammed into his temple, and he hit the sand beneath his feet.

A man said, "All positions disregard that. We checked it out. It's not Wells."

TWENTY

Alana heard the disregard order come over the radio but couldn't let go of the conversation she'd had with Locke just a bit ago. That hadn't been him giving the order to disregard, but she didn't know who it was. She smiled at everyone she'd been talking to and said, "I should go now, get back to work. But thanks for coming to talk to me, you guys."

Hopefully that was enough to placate them into believing she'd done her duty as a "famous person." Not that she only wanted to do the bare minimum, but she was working. People got weird about those they admired acting snooty, but right now she couldn't help it. Not if Locke was in danger.

"Locke." She clicked the button on her radio as she walked down the row of tents. She didn't know where he'd gone, but he had walked off in that direction. "Can you hear me?" When he didn't answer her, she said again, "Locke, do you read?"

Someone replied, but it wasn't Locke's voice. "No extraneous chatter on this line. Let's keep it about work only."

Alana frowned as she walked. How was her asking

if he was there not work? There was definitely something strange going on here, she just didn't know what it was. Or *who* it was. At the end of the row of tents, Alana stood in one spot and looked around. She had no idea where he'd gone.

Okay, God. I guess the only thing I have left is to ask You to help me find him. You know where he is, so tell me where I should go.

She felt kind of silly talking to Him now, considering their lack of rapport. The creator of the universe was certainly able to help, but she didn't know if He would when they'd hardly settled the discord that was between them.

I've been gone for a long time, but I need Your help now. Help me to help Locke, because I don't want to lose him.

Maybe he was fine. She didn't know for sure; she only suspected that something strange was going on. He wasn't responding to radio calls. She kept looking around but didn't know where to start.

"Alana!" Director Matthews trotted over to her, out of breath. Was he the one who had responded to her radio call? She wasn't sure, but it easily could have been him.

"William, do you know where Locke is?"

"I came over to get you. He's asking for your help." William motioned to a tent set back from the others. "Let's go over there now. We should be quick."

Alana drew her weapon, but not because she necessarily thought they were walking into something dangerous. It was more that everything about this was weird. William turned at the door to allow her to go inside first. Locke wouldn't have done that.

She moved the gun by her leg so that he wasn't able to see it and kept him in front of her as she went sideways into the tent.

But for all her cautiousness, Alana did not succeed. The sight of Locke, unconscious on the floor, just caught her heart too much off guard. She rushed to him and knelt by his side, touched his shoulder and turned him over. The wound on the side of his head was red and sticky.

"What happened to him?" She looked back at William, waiting for some kind of explanation. But it was not to be. She'd been right—the person behind this was a Secret Service agent.

And he had his gun on her now.

Alana looked down the barrel, unable to believe that Director Matthews could have betrayed the oath he'd taken this way. Of all people, she never would've believed that he could be the one who would do this.

She lifted her own gun, determined to point it at him the way that he was pointing his at her.

William shook his head. "Don't even think about doing that. Put the gun on the floor and slide it toward me."

He wanted her to disarm? There was no way she was going to do that when this man held his gun on her. "Tell me what's going on. You don't have to shoot me. We can talk about this."

"It's too late for talking, Agent Preston."

"Why did you hurt Locke?"

"Boo-hoo," he said, half laughing. "So sad. I guess the two of you shouldn't have stuck your noses into something that had nothing to do with you."

"Daniel Kaiko tried to kill me, then Brian Wells

tried. Someone messed with our phones and Locke's reports. Explain how that has nothing to do with me," she said.

"It was nothing personal. You have to believe that." William paused. "A well-thought-out plan."

"It seems like your whole plan has been nothing but a bunch of mistakes. Beatrice is dead, and Brian killed Daniel and Zane Franks. Who else has to die?"

Alana didn't want to argue with a man holding a gun on her, but what else was she going to do? Locke was unconscious on the floor behind her and didn't show any signs of coming to anytime soon. At best she needed to stall this man until somebody else figured out what was happening.

She said, "Daniel dragged me into this, and he tried to hurt my sister. So you had Brian Wells kill Daniel before he could tell us anything else. Zane, too. That bomb is Beatrice's design, isn't it? So that in the end it looks like she helped you, but maybe got cold feet, so you killed her."

William smirked. "Not me. There are plenty of players in this game, but I'm hardly one of them."

What if he was the man who had approached Beatrice and Brian? She would have to check his vacation days against the timeline.

Alana wanted to close her eyes right then and thank God. William hadn't known just how close they'd been to figuring out the fact that he was the one behind all this. And they surely would have.

"Why? Why would you do this?" She shook her head. "You're trying to kill the president! Isn't that what you've spent your whole life trying to prevent?"

William began to laugh. "It turns out it's not actu-

ally that easy to do. I guess we really are good at our
jobs. At least until real life comes calling and you find
yourself in the doctor's office." He paused. "They slide
their stool close to you, just to tell you. You have can-
cer. Now there's nothing to do but wait for it to destroy
me from the inside out."

She wanted to weep for him. "I'm so sorry, William.
I had no idea that you were sick."

"That's the whole point," he spat. "No one knows.
And when the marine is done with his part, the president will be alive and I'll be the one who stopped it.
I'll be the one who gave his life to save the man I have
been protecting every day for thirty years."

He wasn't trying to kill the president? He was making it look like a plot...but William was the one who was
going to die? She could hardly wrap her head around
the idea that he wanted to martyr himself because of
his diagnosis.

"You want to die," she said, "instead of fighting?"

"We're all going to die. But I'm not going to let can-
cer take me. I'm the one who gets to choose how I go
out." He patted his chest hard with his free hand. "My
life. My choice."

It was still suicide, no matter what the reason. And
there were just too many variables. Someone was going
to die, and it might not be only William. He could so
easily take out others along with him.

"What about me and Locke?" She paused while her
brain puzzled this out. He seemed to want to kill them,
but what if she could change his mind? "We can tell
everyone your story. That you valiantly gave your life
to save the president."

He sneered a grin. "That's exactly what's going to

happen. I'm going to go down in history as the man who stopped Secret Service agent Preston and director Locke from killing the president."

Locke kept his eyes closed and didn't move. He just lay there listening to everything they said while pain coursed through his head with every pump of his blood. William was crazy! That was the reason the bomb threat had been pinned on him? William had set them up so it looked like they were the ones doing this. He'd orchestrated the whole thing so they were at the center of it all, ready to get it pinned on them. He had to have cohorts everywhere—even in the 9-1-1 system, so that Locke's call had been rerouted.

No one would ever know the truth. A few might suspect things weren't as they seemed, but Locke, Alana and William would be dead. No one would be able to prove that the truth wasn't as William Matthews had designed it.

The rustle of shoes in sand crossed behind him. Locke cracked his eyes open. He'd clue them in to the fact he was awake if he rolled over to look at what was happening in the room, but they'd know sooner or later. He needed to make sure it was at the right time, so that he could subdue William before the bomb went off.

"What are you…?" He hated the fear he heard in Alana's voice.

Locke couldn't wait any longer. He had to stop—

"Everything is ready."

That wasn't William's voice, but it was a man's.

"Brian Wells." Alana gasped his name. *Good girl.* She couldn't know he was awake, but she'd helped him anyway. "Why are you helping him? Why would you betray your country like this?"

"Betray?" His voice reverberated, like he was ready to laugh out loud at her words. "I'm *helping*. This country is entirely too vulnerable. We have to shore up the weaknesses, not ignore them!"

Locke's heart sank. This man wasn't just a hired hand. He believed in what William had sold him and joined the cause. Was he prepared to die, as William was?

"You're both crazy," Alana said. "And I'm not going to stay here and die for *you*."

Locke's heart caught. It was a sharp pain in his chest, a pang of hope that she might be willing to stay here and die for *him*. Maybe he hadn't ruined everything between them. There might still be hope.

If they lived.

"Sit back down," William said. "Or the marine will slit your throat." He paused. "No one will know you didn't die in the explosion."

He heard movement. Then a click of electronics.

"It's done." That was Brian Wells.

"Good."

Someone moved. A scuffle. Alana said, "No," like she was struggling. The gunshot that followed was earsplitting. Alana cried out, and there was a thump. Locke wasn't waiting any longer.

He rolled over. His head swam, and he landed on hands and knees as the world turned a full rotation around him. When he looked up, Alana was clutching her leg with both hands, her eyes wide. The bomb was in the corner of the room on a table. Blinking red.

Locke jumped up and ran toward William to tackle

the man. Locke was unarmed, and William was bringing that gun around to fire at him. But Locke didn't care. William couldn't be allowed to do this.

First he had to stop his colleague.

Then he had to disarm that bomb.

William's eyes hardened as Locke barreled toward him. His lips thinned, and his finger shifted on the trigger. He was going to shoot Locke in the chest.

Brian Wells came out of nowhere and shoved Locke aside. Locke fell to the ground as the gun went off. Brian's body jerked. The marine still punched William, one hard right cross to his head.

William's gun went off one more time as he fell to the ground, unconscious.

Brian stumbled back a step. His hand moved to the front of his shirt, where he'd been shot twice. His legs gave out, and he fell back onto the sand, blinking as though he didn't quite believe it had happened.

He looked at Locke. "I did the right thing finally, didn't I?"

"Yes." He'd saved Locke from being shot and from having to restrain his colleague. Maybe even from having to kill William.

"Tell my daughter I love her."

Locke nodded. He glanced once at Alana. She looked so relieved, her eyes still full of pain from the shot to her leg that she'd suffered. But as much as he wanted to go to her, he couldn't right then. "The bomb."

She nodded. "Take care of it, Locke. And find something to tie up William with."

He'd had some training in defusing ordnances, though it had been basic. If God was truly on his side, then all that staring he'd done at Beatrice's collection of bomb schematics over the years would pay off. If it was her design. She'd shown him where the fail-safe was, said she'd never meant to kill anyone, only send a message to the presidency. It was her knowledge of bombs and chemicals that got her on their watch list.

Locke found the wire, pulled out his multitool and glanced back at Alana. "If this doesn't work and we die, I want you to know that I love you."

She blinked. "Good, because I love you, too." It was matter-of-fact, and he could see the pain in her eyes. It would take more than words to fix this, but he would make sure they had time.

Locke cut the wire, smiling. The blinking red light went dark.

He blew out the breath, tied up William with wire and made his way back over to Alana. "Let's get you some help, okay?"

She nodded. "Okay. You, too." She motioned to his head, which was still bleeding, and winced. "That looks bad."

Locke touched her cheeks. "I want to kiss you, but we should save it for later."

Alana didn't agree, because she pulled his face in with her hands and kissed him. "Thank you for saving all of us, Locke. And I meant what I said. I am in love with you."

Her face was so close her lips whispered against his. Locke kissed her, but only quickly. "Me, too. And you should call me Jay."

Alana's smile was the happiest he'd ever seen on anyone. He had reached for his radio to call for an ambulance and police assistance when the call came.

The president had arrived.

EPILOGUE

One year later

"Ladies and gentlemen, it is my great honor to present to you Mr. and Mrs. James Locke."

The small crowd on the beach clapped and cheered. Locke pulled Alana in close, smiling again at the huge white hibiscus just above her right ear. Before he could kiss her, Alana took the flower from behind her ear and moved it to sit behind her left one. Somehow that made the vows they had just taken all the more meaningful. She was embracing him and no other. Finally they were fully committed to each other, in every aspect of their lives.

Then they kissed.

"Love you, Alana."

She smiled up at him. "Love you, Jay."

When the congratulations died down, Alana turned sideways and they faced every one of their friends and family. Even Kaylee was here, though Mikio had declined to attend.

Sand was getting in Locke's socks, but he didn't care. Alana had told him to wear flip-flops like she was, but there had been no way he would do that. Even if they were getting married on the beach.

Locke's cheeks ached, he was smiling so wide.

They walked down the makeshift aisle between their friends, shaking hands and posing for pictures as they went.

At the end of the aisle stood a sharply dressed Secret Service agent in a black skirt suit and pumps. Now a member of their team, the woman was a friend to both of them.

Alana laughed. "You were supposed to dress beach casual for this, not like you're going to work."

The Secret Service agent shook her head and held out a thick cream-colored envelope. "I got called in for the summit, but the president asked me to get this to the two of you before I left."

Locke nodded. "Thank you."

The back of the envelope held the president's seal. As the woman wandered away, Locke slipped his finger beneath the flap. Inside were two plane tickets and a hotel reservation. Presidential suite. Alana gasped at the destination. "Wow."

Along with it was a card with one word scrawled on it in the president's handwriting.

Congratulations.

* * * * *

*If you enjoyed this book, look for the other titles by
Lisa Phillips, including:*

Available now from Love Inspired Suspense!

Find more great reads at www.LoveInspired.com

Dear Reader,

So often our past defines us. And so often we allow other people's expectations to change the course of our lives. But God's way is freedom. It's life.

In Him we find the fulfillment of all the promise we're unable to drum up in our own lives. His path is so much better, richer, fuller. And it's this grace, this goodness poured out in us that gives us strength to fight against those things that weigh us down.

My prayer for you in reading this book is that God continues to work in you that message of Himself and that you will go forward one more step in the journey.

If you have any comments or questions, feel free to email me at lisaphillipsbks@gmail.com, as I would love to hear from you.

Sincerely,
Lisa Phillips

COMING NEXT MONTH FROM
Love Inspired® Suspense

Available September 5, 2017

TRACKER
Classified K-9 Unit • by Lenora Worth
FBI agent Zeke Morrow is close to capturing his fugitive brother—until his brother's ex-girlfriend and son become the man's targets. Now Zeke and his K-9 partner have a new mission: protect Penny Potter and her little boy at any cost.

POINT BLANK
Smoky Mountain Secrets • by Sandra Robbins
Someone's trying to kill widowed single mother Hannah Riley...and she's not sure why. But with her friend Sheriff Ben Whitman determined to shield her and her daughter from any attempts on their lives, she might just survive long enough to uncover their motive.

THE AMISH WITNESS
by Diane Burke
After witnessing her best friend's murder and returning to her Amish community to hide, Elizabeth Lapp discovers the murderer has followed her. And the only person she can trust to safeguard her is Thomas King, her former love.

REUNITED BY DANGER
by Carol J. Post
Home for their high school reunion, Amber Kingston and her friends receive letters threatening to expose a deadly secret from their past. As her friends are murdered one by one, can Amber work with detective Caleb Lyons to catch the killer in time to stay alive?

TAKEN HOSTAGE
by Jordyn Redwood
When Dr. Regan Lockhart's daughter is kidnapped, the abductors have one demand: she must use her research to create a biological weapon. But with the help of former Delta Force member turned bounty hunter Colby Waterson, can she save her daughter and stop the criminals?

BETRAYED BIRTHRIGHT
by Liz Shoaf
Abigail Mayfield is convinced she left the person threatening her behind when she moved to Texas—until someone breaks into her new home. Now, unable to outrun her stalker, her only option is relying on Sheriff Noah Galloway—a former FBI agent—to crack the case wide-open.

LOOK FOR THESE AND OTHER LOVE INSPIRED BOOKS WHEREVER BOOKS ARE SOLD, INCLUDING MOST BOOKSTORES, SUPERMARKETS, DISCOUNT STORES AND DRUGSTORES.

LISCNM0817

Get 2 Free Books,
Plus 2 Free Gifts —
just for trying the Reader Service!

SPECIAL EXCERPT FROM

Love Inspired.
SUSPENSE

*A single mom must rely on the brother of her rogue
FBI agent ex to keep her son safe.*

*Don't miss TRACKER,
the exciting conclusion to the*
CLASSIFIED K-9 UNIT *series.*

"I'm not leaving without my son."

He pressed the gun against her spine, the cold muzzle chilling against her thin shirt. Late-afternoon sunshine shot over the Elk Basin, giving the vast Montana sky a pastoral rendering. But right now that sky looked ominous.

She didn't want to die here.

Penny Potter twisted around and tried to break free from the man who'd come crashing out of the woods and tackled her just seconds before. Heaving a shuddering breath, she screamed at her former boyfriend, "Jake, there is no way I'm letting you take Kevin out of the country. I told you last time, neither of us is going with you."

Jake Morrow's blue eyes matched the sky but the bitter flash of anger seared Penny's heart. "Yeah, but you took my boy and ran away."

Apprehension and fear gnawed at her but Penny tried to stay calm. She had to keep her head and get back to Kevin before Jake found him. "I told you before, I can't do this. I can't leave the country with you. We're done. They're all looking for you, Jake. Just go and leave us alone."

"*You* might not be willing to come with me," Jake said, his actions filled with a wild recklessness that made her shiver in spite of the late-summer heat. "But my son sure is not staying behind. You're going to take me to him. Now! Or you'll never see him again."

"No!" Penny tried to break away but Jake grabbed her by the collar of her shirt and jerked her back. Praying Kevin was okay, she tried to stay calm so she could see a way out of this. She could only stall him for as long as possible and hope she could somehow escape.

Shoving her ahead of him on the rocky path into the thicket, Jake kept one hand in a death grip on her arm. "Let's go. We're getting Kevin, and either you both go with me or I'll take him and you won't even have time to regret it."

Don't miss
TRACKER by Lenora Worth,
available wherever
Love Inspired® Suspense books and ebooks are sold.

www.LoveInspired.com

LISEXP0817